The Last PyoorBlud

MOLLY LEA

Copyright © 2015 Molly Lea.

All Rights Reserved. No part(s) of this book may be reproduced, distributed or transmitted in any form, or by any means, or stored in a database or retrieval systems without prior expressed written permission of the author of this book.

ISBN: 978-1-62217-484-3

Contents

Chapter 1 1

Chapter 2 9

Chapter 3 14

Chapter 4 23

Chapter 5 32

Chapter 6 36

Chapter 7 40

Chapter 8 48

Chapter 9 58

Chapter 10 66

Chapter 11 75

Chapter 12 84

Chapter 13 99

Chapter 14 111

Chapter 15 118

Chapter 16 125

PART ONE

Chapter 1

On the top of a hill overlooking a valley teeming with overly large houses stood a small café called La Baguette. The owner of the café liked to say that she had picked this spot just so that she would be the highest building on the hilltop, and because it provided a glorious view of the sunset in the afternoon. The light blue tables, coupled with overly large pale pink umbrellas, provided her customers with a welcome place to sit on nice days. On such days a pair of twins, Sarafina and Rhoswen, could be found lounging about after school. Their navy blue and white striped collared sweaters were draped over the back of their chairs; the sweaters were a telltale sign that they belonged to Burgess High School. Identical in every way, the girls each had a unique style to help differentiate themselves. The older twin used chopsticks at every instance, and used a darker eyeliner to accent her warm brown eyes. Her pouty lips were always glossed and she wore no earrings in her slightly tipped ears. Her younger twin, by only five minutes, wore her hair shorter so that it curled around her ears. She wore a pair of large dangling earrings and opted for more muted makeup.

Sarafina reached up to pull the twin chopsticks out of her long brunette hair. The waves cascaded down her back and she let out a sigh.

"Feel better?" Rhoswen asked with a smile. She was reading a textbook, *Anatomy 101*, and sipping a coffee. On the table by her arm was a plate with a half-eaten croissant slathered in strawberry jam.

"You have no clue. Your hair doesn't need to be bound so tightly," Sarafina replied as she ran her hands through her locks. She paused here and there to rub out sore spots on her scalp.

"True enough. Should we get going?" Rhoswen asked.

"I don't know, what's the point in going home now? Tonight is meeting night, Mom and Dad won't be home for hours."

"Yeah, but I still want to get home so that I can start cooking. Besides, you have homework," Rhoswen reminded her sister. Sarafina sent her a glare as she set her hands palms down on the table.

"Fine, can I finish my frappé first?"

"Of course."

The girls lapsed back into silence, each to their own thoughts. Rhoswen wondered if she could get away with writing a term paper on the Illuminati. Sarafina sipped her frappé and absently rubbed her head. She had five different subjects to cover before Wednesday and had only started on two of them. Still she found herself thinking of the mysterious meetings that her parents went to once a month.

"Do you really think they are in the Illuminati?" Sarafina asked suddenly.

Rhoswen wasn't surprised to hear Sarafina saying exactly what she had been thinking.

"No, whatever it is they are doing isn't something so nefarious," Rhoswen said with a smile.

"I don't know, a popular Whig delegate and the head of the Committee for Economic Affairs would be a great addition to an Illuminati faction," Sarafina admitted with a small smile. Rhoswen shook her head at her and laughed. This was a conversation they had all the time while trying to figure out what their parents were doing at their monthly meetings.

"I suppose, but I don't think they are with the Illuminati. Besides, we know that Kit goes to those meetings as well," Rhoswen pointed out. Sarafina nodded in agreement before shrugging.

"It was just a thought. I think I'll ask them tonight after they return when we get to join these meetings."

"Oh don't, Sara. You always end up in a fight. They will tell us when we are ready to join them," Rhoswen said with a sigh. She grabbed her plate and Sarafina's and headed back into the café to dispose of them. Sarafina huffed for a moment before gathering up their things. She handed Rhoswen her book bag when she reemerged and they both turned to walk the short distance down the hill to their house.

~~~

The meeting started out the same way every month. The large group of members filed into one of the elder's houses and congregated in the basement. Each elder had a large dome shaped room with no windows, and together they sat in silence for nearly twenty minutes. It was during this time that Gama and Hilt, parents of Sarafina and Rhoswen, sat in trepidation. The head elder, a woman named Thena had taken an unusual interest in their girls as of late. Gama hoped that she wouldn't bring them up during this meeting, while Hilt simply waited in resigned silence.

"They will be coming of age soon Gama. Have they shown any attributes of the ancestors?" Thena's grave voice pierced the room. The occupants, mainly older men and women with a few youngsters spread throughout the crowd, flinched slightly at the noise. The ritual of silence that preceded every meeting had just finished, as such the air was heavy with the Mother's presence. Thena's voice was like a clap of thunder in such silence. Gama looked stricken before answering.

"No, at least nothing obvious," she replied. Tall and willowy, Gama Thorogana stood proudly next to her short husband. His protruding stomach and balding head often garnered looks of disbelief from people who discovered they were married with children. It was love; that was the only way she could describe the attraction.

"Have you noticed anything where your wife has not, Hilt?" Thena asked. Her eyes were a piercing blue that looked too bright to be held within the confines of such an elderly face. Her white hair was pulled back into a severe bun, and her hands gripped the armrests of her seat in a wrinkled embrace.

"Sarafina enjoys reading by the fire, she uses a wooden stylus that she crafted herself to keep her place, Rhoswen enjoys washing the dishes. They both love to take walks in the forests that surround our land, and I know for a fact that Rhoswen can create works of art from almost any material." Hilt replied. His soft baritone rang out in the stillness of the room. Even the youngest among them stood silently as they listened to this report.

Sighing softly, Thena allowed her eyes to travel upward looking intently at the ceiling. The information was meaningless, nothing mentioned about new abilities, simply a list of habits and hobbies that were unimportant to her.

"Watch them," she stated stiffly.

"As we have for their entire lives, so we shall continue," Gama and Hilt replied in unison. It was a ritualistic statement, one that parents of the Fold responded with when told to watch the progress of their children. Gama could not help but think that the words were truer now than ever before. The rest of the meeting ran smoothly. There was one youth, however, that felt unsettled with Thena's insistence on knowing the welfare of her friends. Kit would just have to make sure they were prepared for when they finally entered the Fold.

~~~

The girls had moved into their own areas of comfort upon getting home. Rhoswen had gone straight to the kitchen to start dinner, while Sarafina had wandered off to their bedroom to get a head start on her homework. After an hour of intense studying, Sarafina waltzed into the living room connected to the kitchen and collapsed into a chair. She watched her sister bustle around cleaning up after dinner for a few minutes before tossing her hair over the back of the chair and settling in to read. The comfortable silence that descended over them did not last very long.

"Stop that," Sarafina exclaimed throwing her hands into the air.

"What?" Rhoswen asked glancing over at her irate twin. Sarafina was glaring at her from her place in front of the fire. She had an open book in her lap and her body had been, until very recently, relaxed and stretched toward the heat. At her exclamation, her hair had tumbled down her back from its resting place atop the chair.

"Stop washing the dishes. That dish is already clean; you have washed it at least three times already. Desist that infernal squeaking at once!" Sarafina exclaimed. She pointed her stylus at her sister to punctuate her point, her eyes bright with passion and agitation. Rhoswen started to giggle, but she did put down the plate she had been washing.

"You know I don't hear the squeaking, Sara." Taking a hand towel from the countertop, Rhoswen walked into the living room drying her hands. She set down the towel on the edge of Sarafina's chair and perched on top of it.

"What are you reading this time?"

"A book about Abraham Lincoln. Did you know he actually hunted vampires?" Sarafina mused looking up with a smirk. Rhoswen smacked her on the arm.

"Oh shut up, you. I think I'll go find myself something to read."

"You have already read everything in the library. Do you plan to start to reread?" Sarafina asked in distaste. She hated rereading a book. She was a firm believer that a book should be enjoyed to the fullest once and then never touched again.

"I haven't read all the books in father's study," Rhoswen said cheekily. She knew what her sister's reaction would be, and was not surprised when outrage and horror appeared on her face.

"We are *not* supposed to go in there without father's permission!"

"And when has that ever stopped either of us from doing exactly as we pleased?" Rhoswen asked as she skipped from the room. She ignored Sara's indignant sputtering and continued through the halls to their father's study. As always, she hesitated for a moment before letting herself into the room. This room, one of her favorites in the house, smelled of old books and cigars. The world globe that sat in one corner was nearly as tall as she was, and the bookshelves that lined the wall behind her father's desk were twice as high. Approaching with caution, she contemplated the selection spread before her. Deciding to look for a book on the shelves she had yet to explore, Rhoswen jumped on the ever-present ladder leaning on the far wall and pushed off. Before running into the opposite wall she grabbed the nearest bookshelf and jerked to a halt. Scrambling to the very top of the ladder she scanned the titles of the books closest to the ceiling. One book caught her attention, a relatively thick volume with no name. Deciding that she could always put it back the next time her father wasn't around if she didn't like it, she grabbed it and climbed down. Pushing the ladder back into place, she quickly exited the room.

"Did you find anything?" Sarafina queried as her sister reentered the living room. Before she could reply, the front door opened. Rhoswen quickly hid the book behind her sister--who gave a surprised squawk--and rushed to the kitchen. There she took out the plates of food from the oven that she had saved for their parents and placed them on the already set table.

"Girls?" their mother's voice rang out.

"In here!" they responded simultaneously.

"Oh good, you saved us something to eat," Gama stated as she walked through the living room, placing a kiss on Sarafina's head before moving into the kitchen. She kissed Rhoswen before settling down to eat. Hilt joined her after completing the same ritual. Both tucked into their meals with hearty enjoyment and Rhoswen smiled with joy.

"So how was the meeting?" Sarafina asked almost casually. Rhoswen shot her a look of disapproval but refrained from saying anything when Sarafina shifted enough so that the edge of the book she had stolen peaked out from behind her back.

"It went as usual," their father said around a mouthful of chicken.

"And usual is?" Sarafina pried yet again.

"Stop your questioning, Sarafina. You know you are forbidden knowledge of the meetings. We have told you time and again, so stop asking!" Gama snapped.

"For how much longer? You have said when we get older we are to become part of these meetings. Well, we are about to turn eighteen! How much older must we get?!" Sarafina shouted, jumping to her feet. Gama opened her mouth to respond, only to be cut off by Hilt.

"Calm yourself this instant, Sarafina. It is not your mother and I who have forbidden you knowledge of our meetings; our instructions come from someone higher than ourselves."

"Who holds such power over you?" Sarafina snapped back. She was tired of being left out of the loop, tired of being told that she was not old enough to know what went on in the monthly meetings that her parents attended. She was expected to one day take over their dynasty, along with her sister; she deserved to know. Besides, if they were working for the Illuminati she wanted to get in on that action.

"That is classified, and you would do well to get used to it," Hilt responded. Sarafina snarled in agitation and grabbed her book, along with Rhoswen's, before storming from the room. Rhoswen stood at her parent's side in silence as they finished their meal, even going so far as to decline her mother's help when they were finished. Instead, she gathered their plates and began to wash them, allowing the flowing water to soothe her frazzled nerves. Before disappearing, Hilt laid a hand on her arm.

"We do not mean to upset you, darling. It simply is not within our power to include you yet," he whispered.

"I know, papa, and truly, though I am curious, I do not mind as much as Sara. I can wait; I have more patience than she does."

"I have always said that you two were perfect opposites," Hilt responded with a chuckle. He gently squeezed her shoulder before exiting the room. And so in the silence that followed Rhoswen was left to her thoughts. She wondered if it had been a trick of the light, or perhaps the way she was angled during the fight, but she was sure that the fire in the hearth had grown hotter and brighter the angrier Sarafina had gotten.

Chapter 2

"You are too impulsive," Rhoswen stated flatly as she entered their bedroom. Sarafina scoffed from her bed and remained silent. The muted green and yellow wallpaper always reminded Rhoswen of the forest behind their house. The setup of the room was one that the sisters had feuded over for a long time, but the dorm-like staging of the room had suited them both in the end.

"How are you not driven as mad as I am by the blatant lack of trust?" Sarafina asked after a moment.

"I know that mother and papa are keeping secrets from us, but what right do we have to know them? You cannot honestly tell me that you think these meetings have anything to do with our inheritance. No, whatever it is that they discuss in those meetings, it is more than something as simple as money," Rhoswen said as she settled onto her own bed. Sarafina had placed the book she had stolen on her pillow. Gingerly she picked it up and brought it over to her desk.

"Do you really think so?" Sarafina asked hesitantly. Rhoswen glanced over to see her propped up on one arm. Her gaze was unwavering and Rhoswen felt a slight shiver crawl up her spine. Though genetically identical, she had always thought that her sister possessed all the passion that she lacked. Her eyes would sometimes burn with a fire so intense, like now, that it was hard to meet them.

"I know so. Don't ask me how, I just do. There is more to all of this than our financial situation, more than just rubbing shoulders with the other most influential families. Today when you asked who had more power over us…"

"Yes, what about it?" Sarafina inquired.

"I think that is what you should be thinking about. Mother and Father have great power in their own right. There can't be too many people who have more," Rhoswen concluded. Seeing that she had given her sister something to think about, she finally turned her attention to the book in her hands. Opening it to the first page she encountered the most elegant scrawl she had ever seen.

Antiquissimus est matris in
Cognition creaturarum.
Omnes Pyoorblud

"Oh wow, this book must be old!" Rhoswen exclaimed in excitement.

"Why do you say that?" Sarafina asked. Her voice spoke of her agitation; apparently Rhoswen had broken her concentration.

"The inscription is in Latin, it reads: *Within lies the knowledge of the oldest of the Mother's Creations. All are Pyoorblud.* That is a very strange way to spell pureblood even for Latin," Rhoswen mused. When Sarafina made no reply Rhoswen simply shrugged it off. She quickly flipped through the rest of book to make sure it wasn't all in Latin. Not that she didn't want to know what it said, but it had been at least four years since she had studied Latin. She felt that her knowledge was too rusty to attempt to read an entire book written in the dead language. Sighing softly, she realized that it was in English. Settling into a more comfortable position, she opened to the first page and began to read.

The Last PyoorBlud

~~~

The air that fluttered through the open window of the downstairs sunroom brought with it the smell of lavender blossoms and cigarette smoke. The husband and wife had retired to this room, which also served as Gama's study, directly after dinner to discuss their children away from prying eyes and ears.

"Did you see what I saw?" Hilt asked. Gama sat on the ledge of one of the room's four large windows and watched the thin trail of smoke rise from her cigarette into the night.

"The fire," Gama sighed.

"Yes the fire--the angrier she got the hotter it burned. It was nearly white by the time she stormed from the room. She obviously has the signs!" Hilt exclaimed with joy.

"And Rhoswen, did she show any signs tonight?"

"I do not believe she noticed it, but when I stopped to say goodnight I saw that she was washing dishes again."

"What is so miraculous about that?" Gama snapped.

"The faucet was not turned on my dear, and yet the water ran," Hilt explained. Gama stared at him with wide eyes. She did not know where his joy was coming from. The news that their daughters had indeed inherited abilities through their bloodlines was distressing to her. Especially considering what their next course of action would have to be.

"We will have to report this; Thena will want to know immediately," Gama whispered.

"Give it some time. This is only the first time that we have witnessed it, and as neither girl took notice of it, it is still too soon to inform them of this part of their inheritance," Hilt argued.

"Fire and water, complete opposites and yet they are exactly the same. How do they complete each other so well when they each have the power to destroy the other? This could be very dangerous, Hilt. I can see why Thena is so worried," Gama said, chewing on the end of her cigarette.

"Can you also see why I have become more and more wary of her? We have not had children enter the Fold with such strong ties to the Mother in over a millennia. What purpose could Thena want with them?" Hilt muttered. He paced the room with one hand twirling his own cigar. He had given up smoking years ago, but to have the thick cancer stick in his hands provided a relief that he didn't think he would ever be able to replicate.

"What do you mean? They are to be invited into the Fold just as the others have been. They will be expected to attend ceremonies, and when they have built up their own reputations and notability they will do as we all do, bring glory to the Mother," Gama said.

"Yes, that is what I thought as well, but I have heard some very disturbing things, my dear. For instance, it was brought to my attention that Rayne has gone missing." Hilt had paused beside her at the window, his mouth pulled into a deep frown.

"Rayne has gone missing! Why were we not informed of this at the meeting? And how did you find out?" Gama exclaimed.

"I have my sources, which I cannot reveal to you at this time; and that is the question isn't it, why were we not informed? When someone with Rayne's potential goes missing you would think that Thena would sound the alarm even before the meeting. And yet we talked of the girls intensely and then of meaningless dribble. Not a word spoken about our missing prodigy."

"You fear Thena?" Gama asked after a few moments of silence.

"I fear her, yes. I fear her greatly, but not for the reasons you might believe. She has been head for many, many years, and her eyes are very bright, brighter than they should be for her age. Gama my darling, she looked half crazy when Rayne was brought into the Fold, do you remember her smile?" Hilt sighed trying to squash the shiver that resulted from his words. Gama suppressed her own shiver. Thena's face had split into a grin so wide it contorted her face into something ugly. Her eyes had gleamed with an inner fire, and her skin seemed to crackle with an intense electricity that all could feel.

"I remember…vividly."

"I fear that she is not what she has made herself out to be. Her ancestors must be much more sinister in nature."

"You cannot be insinuating that she is a descendent of *them*!" Gama snapped sharply. Hilt simply looked at her, his face grave.

"You cannot be sure," Gama begged, her voice dropping to a frightened whisper.

Hilt sighed and flopped inelegantly into the nearest chair. "I wish I could say I wasn't, but with each piece of information I receive I fear there is no other conclusion to make. Though the Mother calls them our perfect other, the destruction they brought upon us was something no one could have imagined. They nearly drove us to extinction. Somewhere in her blood, Thena holds the attributes of our most hated foe. She must be from a very old line, back when we thought there was no other choice. Before humans were considered and we mated with…"

"Don't say it!" Gama motioned for him to stop, but it was too late; Hilt breathed the words with all the fear that they deserved.

"*Dark Fairies.*"

The silence that followed was heavier than any silence they had experienced during a meeting. Meeting her husband's eyes, Gama could not help but wonder if they had just called down demons upon their household.

Chapter 3

Thena made her way slowly down the spiraling staircase that lead from the main floor of her prestigious mansion to the basement. This level of the house was hardly ever visited by anyone other than the members of the Fold, and that was only once a month. Thena passed by the large room that the meetings were held in and walked further into the basement. In the farthest northern corner there were a series of rooms that only a few knew existed. Taking a large brass key out of her pocket, she unlocked one of the many doors that lined the corridor.

"Hello, Rayne. How are you this evening?" Thena asked, her voice soft with concern. The girl residing in the room before her stood with her back to Thena and remained silent. Thena stood for a moment before frowning deeply.

"Now, Rayne--there is no need for you to act like this. You only have to agree to help with this glorious mission, and you will be allowed to leave and go back to your home," Thena lied. She paused for a moment, waiting for a response, but Rayne only stiffened her shoulders and refused to budge. "You need to let me in. You will not bar me from entering, understand." Thena commanded. Her voice had not risen in volume, but Rayne's shoulders hunched as if a great weight had settled upon them.

"No. Let me out of here, Thena," she whispered. Her back was still facing the doorway. She did not want Thena to see that she had already picked the lock of one of the chains that kept her bound to this room. Sensing Thena about to enter the room, Rayne quickly commanded the floor to block her way. The earth under her feet heeded her command and rose up into a wall blocking Thena's entry. Rayne had never been so happy to be able to control Earth. She also praised the Mother that Thena's house's foundation was old and made directly into the Earth, instead of with cement on top like so many others.

"GIRL!" Thena screeched as she was thrown back by the force of the wall rising to stop her passage. Picking herself up off the floor, she stared in fury at the girl on the other side of the door. Now that she felt no danger of Thena's entry, Rayne had allowed the floor to return to its initial position.

"You will not come in here, and I will not be kept here for much longer," Rayne snarled over her shoulder. Thena simply huffed in annoyance before slamming the door and locking the girl in once more. She turned back to the staircase and marched away as fast as her limbs would allow. Once she had reached her room, Thena let out a terrific scream of fury.

"You allow her to rile you up too easily. Patience, my dear," a soft voice spoke. Thena whirled to face the man leaning casually against her bed. He was tall, his auburn hair trailing down his back to sway gently against the back of his thighs. Obviously elfish from the tilt of his eyes and the point of his ears, he stood with an authority that anyone would notice.

"Hine, what are you doing here?" Thena asked as she approached him cautiously. She was not overly fond of this particular ally. He was shady, he had far too much power and influence and he knew it. He had employed Thena's help, citing their ancient ancestors as a link between them. Thena had thought to refuse him until he told her the name of his grandmother, the most powerful dark fairy of her age. Now as she stood in his shadow, Thena tried not to let her resentment and hatred of him show on her face.

"I have come to see how you have progressed with our young detector. Obviously, from your infuriated scream, things have not progressed much, if at all," Hine replied. Pushing off from the bed, he stood in front of Thena at his full height, shadowing her.

"She does not want to be used, and she has too much power," Thena mumbled.

"More than you I suppose, but she possesses less power than I hold in my pinkie finger. I can make her do what I want."

"Then why don't you!" Thena exclaimed. She stared up into Hine's face in defiance, but shrank back under the weight of his stare.

"I do not want to tip my hand so soon, cousin. This is not the only avenue on which I travel. To reveal myself now would be…foolish," Hine explained. He sounded condescending, as if he were explaining himself to a child.

"I cannot force her. You are right she is more powerful than I. Age has weakened me, and I admit, I should not have told her of her purpose here," Thena grumbled. She stumbled backward when Hine rounded on her.

"You what?!" he exclaimed. His eyes were wide with disbelief; surely this woman was not foolish enough to tell the girl they intended to use her. Hine had never seen a manifestation of the Mother's gifts so powerful in one child. This one girl had every ability to a point and she could detect latent abilities in others. She was to have been the key to his plan, and now this daft woman had set him back weeks, if not months, in his plans.

"I simply told her that she would be serving a higher function within the Fold. That she would be doing a greater service to the Mother if she assisted in the locating of those children with latent ancestral traits," Thena stuttered.

"You told her that we wanted to use her. You are as stupid as you are arrogant!" Hine spat.

"How is what I said wrong? You told me to convince her. She has been a devoted follower since her induction. I was sure that telling her such a thing would convince her."

"And instead she wants nothing to do with us, and as I cannot show myself at this time and force her to do my bidding you have rendered her useless to me. Never mind, there will be others like her. Ship her out on the next boat headed to the Americas. And make sure she stays there," Hine hissed into Thena's frightened face. He waited for her to nod her consent before striding out the door. Thena stood, still in shock and horror.

"The Americas…" Thena whimpered. In truth, none of those who resided in her Fold that were close to her in age had ever traveled to the Americas, and so the horror stories that had reached their ears had turned it into a place of darkness and death, regardless of the truth. Though time had surely changed the Americas, Thena quaked in fear at the mere mention of the place.

~~~

Rhoswen stared down at the last page of the miraculous book that she had stumbled across. If she hadn't seen the things she had seen the night before with her own eyes, she would have chalked the entire book up as a work of fiction. But it made sense, Sarafina's fiery attitude and spirit, and the way that the fire seemed to burn brighter the night before. All of these things led Rhoswen to the conclusion that her sister was a nymph. Rhoswen sat in indecision…how was she to test her theory?

"Sarafina, you will never believe what I have discovered in this book," Rhoswen exclaimed as she dropped down onto her sister's bed. Sarafina groaned in annoyance and turned over to face her.

"Is it really that important that you have to wake me up?" Sarafina mumbled.

"Oh hush, it is well past noon already. This is what happens when you stay up all night," Rhoswen scolded.

"Exactly, and since the light at your desk was still on when I did finally go to sleep myself, I can only assume that you still have not gone to sleep," Sarafina struggled into a seated position. She studied the bags underneath Rhoswen's eyes and stifled a sigh.

"What have you found?"

"This book is like a wildlife guidebook, only the creatures that it talks about in here are fictional. At least that is what I thought, but the more I read about them the more it seemed to fit. I mean you are constantly next to the fire, you can make absolutely everything grow, better even than mother. You get angry and the fire burns brighter, it all fits!" Rhoswen exclaimed practically bouncing with joy. Sarafina simply stared at her in confusion.

"Dearest, that made no sense. Maybe you should go to sleep and try to explain it to me again when you are more lucid," Sarafina gently stated, attempting to guide her sister to her own bed.

"No, you don't understand, Sara. I'm telling you that I think you are one of the creatures in this book. You are a nymph!" Rhoswen huffed in annoyance.

"How dare you. I am not some mythical monster!" Sarafina drew up in offense. To hear her sister accuse her of being a nymph was just hurtful.

"No, you twit. It's not a bad thing. Oh just look," Rhoswen flipped the book open to the page she had bookmarked and held it out for Sarafina to read.

Nymph:

An Elemental being that communes with the Mother (Mother Earth) through the use of any or all of the four elements. Most nymphs have the overall control of a single element such as Fire or Water. There are few exceptions where a nymph may have marginal control over all four elements. It is even rarer to encounter a nymph who has full control over two elements.

Many nymphs are now hybrids due to their fraternization with humans and other elemental creatures, such as elves or fairies.

"I don't understand. You think that I am this creature?" Sarafina asked, her voice filled with confusion.

"I'm sure of it, but we could always test it," Rhoswen said with a smile. She was glad that her sister was at least considering the possibility now.

"Oh really, and how do you propose we do that?" Sarafina asked placing the book down on her bed. She stood in front of her sister with her hands on her hips.

"I'll show you," Rhoswen huffed. She spun on her heel and disappeared out the door. She was only gone for a few moments before she returned, a small box clutched tightly in one hand and a small potted plant in the other.

"What have you got there?" Sarafina asked peering at the objects.

"It's a matchbox. I borrowed it from mother's study. And this is a plant from the hallway. I want you to take a match and light it on fire," Rhoswen stated, offering the box to her sister. Sarafina scoffed and grabbed the matchbox. She pulled out a single match and struck it against the strip on the side of the box.

"I don't see what that proved," Sarafina stated calmly as she shook out the match. Rhoswen resisted the urge to smack her in the back of the head; it would not have been dignified.

"Sarafina, I want you to light the match with your mind. Will the fire to start, and do not use the strip."

"Of all the utter nonsense... there is no way I can do that," Sarafina sputtered. Rhoswen grabbed the matchbox back and withdrew a single match.

"Light it on fire."

"I cannot simply light a match on fire with my mind. This is the real world; this is the 21st century, not some made up fantasy!" Sarafina objected.

"Light the match on fire," Rhoswen insisted.

"I tell you I cannot. There is no possible way for me to light that match on fire without touching it in some way," Sarafina protested again. Rhoswen narrowed her eyes in frustration and shoved the match under Sarafina's nose.

"Just light the bloody match already and stop being such a twat!" she yelled. As the words left her mouth Sarafina snarled at her in response and the match caught on fire. They stared at it incredulously for a moment before Sarafina shrieked and Rhoswen began to laugh.

"I told you, you could do it," Rhoswen chuckled.

"What--who--how...?" Sarafina sputtered. Wanting to strike while the iron was hot, Rhoswen picked up the plant and dropped it into Sarafina's hands.

"Make it grow. And don't tell me you can't until you try," Sarafina stared at her sister and then the plant, still in shock from the match. Looking at the plant she simply thought that she could use a flower to smell at that moment. Both girls watched as the single bud on the stalk grew in size before gently opening to reveal its soft purple center. The girls watched in awe as the flower bloomed and Sarafina looked even more shocked than she had before. Finally feeling the lack of sleep catching up with her, Rhoswen decided to take a nap.

Rhoswen reached over and picked up the book from Sarafina's bed. Gently she pressed it into her hands.

"Here, dear sister--read up. I am going to bed," Rhoswen grinned. With that said she returned to her side of the room and crawled under the covers, leaving her stupefied sister frozen in the middle of the room. The only part of Sarafina that moved were her eyes which traveled from the matchbox to the book to the flower pot and back.

~~~

The short redhead bounced up the stairs of the mansion and sighed before knocking on the door. She had spent days after the meeting determining what she would say to the twins the next time she saw them. Should she warn them about Thena's interest in them, or should she allow their parents to take care of it? Kaywinnet sighed again as she waited for the door to open.

"Ah, Miss Bennett--the family was just sitting down for dinner. Would you like to come in?" the butler Yessi asked as he opened the door to admit her.

"Only for a few moments, I know that Rhoswen will try to feed me," Kaywinnet said with a smile as she slipped past him. She walked down the familiar hallways humming as she went.

"Hello all, how have you been today?" Kaywinnet announced herself as she entered the dining room. All of the occupants in the room turned to her.

"KIT!" Rhoswen and Sarafina exclaimed together. They pushed from the table and rushed the older girl. Laughing at their excitement, Kaywinnet hugged them back.

"Hello, girls. How are you guys on this fine day?"

"Well I have been fine, but Rhoswen has been washing dishes all day," Sarafina stated casually. Rhoswen sent her sister a glare before looking sheepishly down at Kaywinnet.

"What is wrong my dear? You only wash when something is on your mind," Kaywinnet stated as she lowered her voice. Obviously Rhoswen was uncomfortable discussing whatever was on her mind in front of her parents.

"We shall talk about it later," Kit whispered. Rhoswen nodded before smiling.

"Come eat with us, Kit."

"Yes do come and eat with us, we have not seen you in some time," Gama commented lightly. She was glad to see Kaywinnet; in fact she was looking forward to getting to talk to her about her thoughts on Thena.

"I would love to eat with you. I'm sure Rhoswen has made more than enough for me to steal," Kaywinnet said with a smile, heedless of the contradiction Yessi heard in her statement. The butler backed out of the room as silently as he had come, having already correctly interpreted that Kaywinnet would be staying for dinner and set a place and plate at the table for her.

"After dinner I would like to talk to you. Hilt and I both would actually," Gama stated a few moments later.

"Well actually, I was hoping to talk to the girls," Kaywinnet spoke quickly.

"Oh there will be time for that afterward, I am sure. In any case, I will have Yessi set up your room for you. You can stay the night here, and if nothing else you can talk to the girls later," Gama waved away her concern with her fork. Kaywinnet exchanged a glance with Rhoswen who shrugged.

"Of course, ma'am," Kaywinnet agreed.

Chapter 4

Kaywinnet restrained herself from pacing the confines of Gama's office. She was desperate to have this meeting over and done with so that she could go talk to Rhoswen. Taking no notice of her hosts, she continued to fidget in agitation.

"Kit, I have a very important question for you," Gama's voice finally penetrated through her frustrated mind.

"Yes, ma'am?" Kaywinnet responded sitting up straighter in her chair. It was only then that she noticed the weary and hesitant expressions on both Gama and Hilt's faces.

"When was the last time you talked to Rayne?" Hilt asked. He knew his wife wanted to ask the girl about Thena, but he wanted to see just how deeply the old woman's deception went first.

"I talked to her a couple of days before the last meeting. She had told me that she was excited about something," Kaywinnet paused for a moment as she tried to remember. "Something to do with a new assignment from Thena, I believe."

"An assignment from Thena, did you say?" Hilt asked leaning forward. Kaywinnet nodded hesitantly as she watched Gama and Hilt exchange a grave look in confusion.

"Is something wrong? I didn't see her at the meeting, but I just assumed that she had gotten an assignment that required her immediate attention," Kaywinnet prodded gently.

"That is something we have yet to discover for ourselves; however, your information does shed some light on the situation. If you will excuse me…" Hilt stated absently as he rose from his seat and left the room.

"Ma'am?"

"I want to know your honest opinion on Thena, Kaywinnet. After you tell me what you think of her--and be totally honest my dear, this is important--you should still have time to see the girls before they retire," Gama stated with a sigh. She sat behind her desk with her fingers crossed.

"I think, well I think she…" Kaywinnet paused unable to go on. She had known this family since she was very young, and as such trusted them immensely. But her thoughts about Thena were anything but benevolent, and she wondered if it really would be wise to speak her mind.

"You have nothing to fear my dear, just tell me what you think," Gama encouraged. Taking a deep breath and deciding to trust the woman who was like a second mother to her, Kaywinnet responded.

"I think she is secretive and manipulative. I think she has ulterior motives for more than half of the things that she does, and I also think that her fascination with your children these last few meetings is something to be concerned about."

Gama sat silently for a moment and regarded Kaywinnet with a closed off expression. Finally, a small smile graced her features, relieving the tension Kaywinnet hadn't been aware was building between them.

"I think you just might be right. We shall have to keep a close eye on them," Gama stated quietly, almost as if she were talking to herself. Kaywinnet sat still for a few more moments before she was waved away by her hostess.

"Goodnight, Gama," Kaywinnet stated as she crossed the room to the door.

"Goodnight, my dear. Tell the girls that they are not to stay up past dawn again. I could have sworn I saw a light on in their room very early this morning," Gama replied.

Kaywinnet chuckled, "I'll be sure to let them know," and exited the office, softly shutting the door behind her.

~~~

The girl being led up the neighboring gangplank covered in chains held a unique fascination for Foster. He stood at his impressive height of 6'8," legs spread apart to support his stance on the gently rocking ship, and hands crossed leisurely behind his back. As he observed the girl, a small thing with braids and a stubborn albeit slightly terrified look on her face, he nodded at regular intervals to his companion.

"—and for the love of all that is Holy, do not let that cargo be sold for under 6,000 pounds. Foster!" The small brunette at his side exclaimed.

"I can hear you fine, darling," Foster calmly stated.

"Then what did I just tell you?" the woman asked. Tearing his gaze from the girl that was being led below deck on the ship next door, Foster peered down into the beautiful mismatched eyes of his wife.

"You said you were going to shore with Rubella, though god knows what trouble you two will get into. You also stated that you planned to go to the pub and have a drink, or four or five, and try to see if any new shipments are leaving within the next few days. While you are gone I, along with the rest of the crew, are to sell the cargo we already possess for no less than 6,000 pounds. Did I miss anything?" Foster asked, a small smile tugging at his lips. His wife, Nadia, stared up at him with a scowl.

"How do you do that?" she asked with a huff.

"Do what, my darling?" Foster asked once again turning his attention back to the neighboring ship.

"THAT! Pay no attention to me and yet hear and comprehend everything I have to say," Nadia exclaimed, her hand coming up to wave in front of his face. Catching the hand with one quick movement Foster brought it to his mouth with a smile.

"Practice, my dearest. I have simply had a long time to practice. Now if you expect to drink Rubella under the table I suggest you get going. She has probably already beaten you to the pub."

"I said I was going to have ONE drink," Nadia repeated, even as a smile tugged at her own lips. Her husband tended to be quite adorable sometimes.

"Yes, and you and I both know that once a challenge is issued it will be more than one drink that you actually consume. Just try not to get carried away, hmm…" Foster requested. He laughed as Nadia punched him in the arm, quickly grabbing her by the waist to lay a kiss on her before releasing her.

"Now be gone, wench, so that I may sell your booty!" Foster exclaimed.

"Never speak like that again," Nadia said with a laugh, "And don't forget who the captain of this ship is!"

"Aye, aye, Captain!" Foster said with a mock salute. Nadia smiled up at him before making her way off the ship. Once she was halfway down the docks, Foster turned his attention once again to the ship next door. That girl had looked familiar, and he thought that Britain was no longer condoning the trading of slaves. He itched to investigate, but he had been given orders.

"Right, well onwards and upwards," he muttered before lifting his voice to call out to the rest of the men and women that comprised the crew. They had some stolen goods to sell.

~~~

Kaywinnet made her way down one of the many hallways in the mansion toward the twins' bedroom. She knew that they had been offered their own rooms many times before and that they had grabbed at the opportunity. Yet years later, they found themselves rooming together once more. Stopping outside of the large oak doors, Kaywinnet raised a hand and knocked gently.

"Come in," Sarafina called. Kaywinnet opened the door and took in the scene before her. Both girls were squared off in the center of the room. Sarafina seemed to be brandishing a book at Rhoswen who simply stood glaring at her sister.

"Oh, Kit--thank goodness you have arrived. Maybe you can talk some sense into this stubborn mule of a woman!" Sarafina exclaimed, throwing the book she had been brandishing onto Rhoswen's bed.

"You needed to talk to me, Rhoswen?" Kaywinnet asked, choosing to ignore Sarafina for a moment.

Rhoswen looked hesitant for only a moment before turning to collect the book that Sarafina had thrown on her bed.

"I know I'm not supposed to, but I was bored, so I went and got a book from Father's study, and it had the most amazing information inside. When I finally finished reading it, well I just knew that Sarafina had to be one so we tried it and it worked. But now she wants to go tell everyone, which I for one think is a horrible idea, and she wants to find others like her, which I think is an even worse idea, and I just wanted to know what you thought..." Rhoswen's words tumbled over each other as she attempted to talk without breathing. Kaywinnet stood for a moment to let the sentences digest.

"What was in the book?" she finally settled on asking.

"My heritage, well actually our heritage, although mule over there doesn't think it could be related to her as well," Sarafina interjected before Rhoswen could say a word. Rhoswen opened her mouth to argue before snarling and shoving the book into Kaywinnet's hands.

"Pages 135-148 talk about nymphs. They are a sort of magical race from long ago. My theory was that Sarafina was a decedent of these creatures, and so we tested my theory and I proved to be correct. She had control over fire. We tested it with a match a few days ago. Sarafina seems to think that I hold the same powers that she does, but we have tested it and I have shown no signs. She just refuses to stop insisting.

I refuse to tell mum and papa, because really what can you even say… but this twit wants to shout to the whole world about it!" Rhoswen explained as Kaywinnet flipped to the correct pages and read. The more she read the wider her eyes got. So the girls knew about their heritage; that actually saved her some trouble.

"Why wouldn't you also be a nymph Rhoswen? I mean you are Sarafina's twin. Don't you think that if she were one, so too would you be?" Kaywinnet asked carefully after closing the book.

"Well I thought so, but I don't have control over fire," Rhoswen stated with a frown.

"Just because you are twins does not mean that you will have the same affinity. And what do you mean you tried it?!" Kaywinnet suddenly exclaimed. "Do you know how dangerous that is? What if something had gone wrong? Especially if Sarafina's affinity is with fire; fire is the most unpredictable gift the Mother can bestow upon a person!" Kaywinnet exclaimed rounding on Sarafina. Sarafina simply grinned at her and picked up a match.

"Wanna see?" She asked dropping into the non-formal speech she always seemed to develop around Kit.

"Of course!" Kaywinnet exclaimed. She blushed when the girls laughed at her abrupt about-face but continued to look at Sarafina with anticipation. Sarafina smirked at her before turning her attention to the match in her hand. She concentrated, her eyes screwing up and her mouth became pinched, and just as perspiration appeared on her forehead Rhoswen whispered, "Oh get on with it, you silly twit!" As the words left her mouth the match lit. Sarafina glared at her sister before turning a beaming smile toward Kaywinnet.

"Interesting, so you can only manifest it if you are angry or annoyed," Kaywinnet muttered as she studied the match.

"Well, it is fire; I just assumed that something so volatile needed an emotion just as strong," Rhoswen stated calmly from behind her. Sarafina shook out the match with a frown.

"That would usually be the case, but Sarafina can not only manipulate fire that already exists, she can also manifest it. Not many of us have that power," Kaywinnet stated. She then winced as both girls gasped at her.

"YOU ARE A NYMPH?!" They exclaimed together. Kaywinnet shrugged as she nodded.

"Why didn't you tell us?" Sarafina demanded.

"I didn't think you needed to know. I'm actually part nymph; I have more elven blood than nymph," Kaywinnet admitted.

"So what does that mean?" Rhoswen asked as she started frantically flipping through the book. She came upon the chapter on Elves and began to read aloud.

> *There are six kinds of Elvin bloodlines: mountain, plains, forest, water, dark, and desert elves. As their names would suggest, each Elvin line carries characteristics of its homeland.*

"'Characteristics of its homeland,' but what does that mean?" Sarafina interrupted. Rhoswen shot her sister a glare, but Kaywinnet cut in before an argument could start.

"It means that, for people like me who contain woodland/forest Elvin blood, we have abilities that would help us survive in our chosen habitat. For instance, I am very good with animals, I can actually communicate with most of them; I'm good at starting fires the old fashion way, and I always know when we are close to water. It also means that I am an excellent hunter and a pretty decent shot with a bow and arrow, if I do say so myself," Kaywinnet ended with a laugh. The girl's faces had developed a quality of awe that was slightly disturbing.

"What?" Kaywinnet finally asked.

"That is amazing. I didn't know you could do all that!" Sarafina exclaimed. Rhoswen nodded her agreement.

"Well, when I was growing up my parents taught me, especially when I started showing the signs."

"Signs of what?" Rhoswen asked.

"Signs of maturity," Kaywinnet explained. "It means that I was starting to show my abilities. It is the same with you. Now that you have started to show your abilities you will be invited into the Fold with the rest of us."

"The Fold? Is that where mum and papa go on these monthly meetings?" Rhoswen asked quickly catching on.

"Yes, I have been a member since I was sixteen, after the first year of my maturity. If you are exhibiting the signs now, that means you will be invited in next year at this time," Kaywinnet confirmed with a smile. Rhoswen was a very smart girl, she couldn't help but think.

"Why a whole year though?" Sarafina asked in frustration. She was slightly disappointed that her parents were not part of the Illuminati; however, being part of a secret organization of mythical creatures was a nice second choice.

"Because you have to learn to control your abilities before you can enter the Fold. Once a member, you will be expected to do your part for our community. We can't have you setting people on fire," Kaywinnet replied dryly.

"I would never set anyone on fire!" Sarafina exclaimed. As she yelled she threw a hand up in the air in aggravation. Rhoswen gasped and Kaywinnet took a small step back.

"Sarafina calm down now!" Kaywinnet commanded as her eyes stayed glued to Sarafina's still raised hand.

"Sara, please calm down," Rhoswen begged in a hushed whisper.

"What, what's wrong now?" Sarafina asked lowering her arm. As her hand came into view, she stopped to stare at it in horror. Her entire hand was ablaze.

"BLOODY HELL! My hand, why is my hand on fire?!" Sarafina shrieked. Kaywinnet and Rhoswen watched in horror as the fire slowly started to creep up Sarafina's arm the more frantic she became. Finally, unable to watch any longer Rhoswen rushed to her sister's aid.

"NO!" Kaywinnet yelled attempting to grab Rhoswen as she passed. She missed by inches and could only watch in horror as Rhoswen grabbed Sarafina's burning arm.

HISSSSSSSSSSSS

Rhoswen slowly opened the eyes she had shut upon grabbing her sister's arm. She stared down at the once burning arm in surprise and wonder. The fire had been put out, not by smothering as she had attempted to do, but by water--water that was even now encircling her hands in a liquid cocoon. Backing away, Rhoswen let go of Sarafina's arm, which was now dripping, small tendrils of smoke whisking off it like the smoke from her mother's cigarettes.

"What in the world?" Rhoswen whispered. Kaywinnet came to stand beside her and upon seeing what had put the fire out started to laugh.

"Well I guess we know which ability you inherited," she said with a laugh. Rhoswen relaxed at the sound of her laughter and turned back to Sarafina. Sarafina was glancing between her arm and Rhoswen's hands. Then, quite unexpectedly, she burst into tears. Rushing forward Rhoswen once again wrapped her sister in her arms. This time, however, both hands were dry.

Chapter 5

Rubella walked in a slightly tilting way down the dock. She paused for a moment when her ship came into view and glanced around. She knew she was forgetting something, so she simply waited for her drunken brain to catch up with her.

"You daft bird. You left me at the pub again!" a slurred voice called out from behind her. Rubella's face split with a grin as she turned to see her friend and captain staggering up behind her.

"Nadia! I knew I had forgotten something," Rubella muttered. "What's ta-taking you so long? Walk on, my dear captain, walk on!" Rubella exclaimed pointing toward their ship. She threw her hands out so exuberantly that she toppled forward with the momentum. Nadia caught her just in time; unfortunately they both still ended up in a pile on the ground.

"Foster is going to have my hide," Nadia mumbled as she dragged Rubella into a standing position once again.

"Pish posh, he adores you. Just make it back to the ship in one piece and he will take care of the rest. And make sure you don't leave me," Rubella scowled at her friend.

"So says the woman who left me to pick up the tab back at the pub. I won our little game; you should have picked up the tab," Nadia grumbled.

"Never you mind that, just get me to my bed," Rubella muttered. Nadia muttered to herself the rest of the way to the ship. As they reached the gangplank, she stopped for a moment.

"Was the matter?" Rubella slurred. The alcohol was hitting her hard now and she was having trouble keeping herself upright.

"I can't walk up the plank with you hanging off of me like this. Can you make it on your own?" Nadia stated after a moment of silence.

"No."

Nadia sighed before staring at the plank again in annoyance. Why did the damn thing have to sway with the boat?

"Alright hold on. I'll go get Warren. Or maybe Foster would be better," Nadia stated as she set her friend down at the bottom of the plank. Rubella simply slumped over to the side and closed her eyes. Nadia stared down at her for a moment before nodding and quickly, as quickly as her legs and head would allow, walking up the gangplank.

"FOSTER!" She shouted from the top of the steps leading below deck. She only had to wait a moment before her husband appeared at the bottom of the staircase.

"What happened?" He simply asked as he made his way to her.

"You were right--I drank Rubella under the table, and then some. She is stuck at the bottom of the gangplank. I can't bring her onboard. I barely made it up the plank myself without falling off of it. Would you be a dear and go get her for me? Just hand her off to Warren, he'll know what to do with her." With that and a short kiss to his cheek, Nadia stumbled into their bedroom. Foster stood for a moment simply shaking his head at his wife's drunken state.

"Warren?" Foster called over his shoulder quietly. Warren, the ship's medic, stepped out of the shadows with a small grin.

"I'll get her," he stated simply as he passed Foster to retrieve his mate.

"Rubella?" He spoke softly as he reached her slumped form.

"I had too much to drink," Rubella mumbled as she turned her head at the sound of his voice. Warren chose not to comment and instead he simply bent and gathered her into his arms. Rubella moaned in protest before settling her head on Warren's shoulder.

"You always drink too much," Warren whispered into her hair. She snorted at him and simply smiled. Warren bore her to their bedroom and gently laid her down.

"Will there be anything else, my love?" Warren asked softly as he stared down into her sleepy features.

"No, but tomorrow I have to write a letter. Don't let me forget..." Rubella mumbled as she started to drift off.

"To who?" Warren enquired not sure if she had heard him.

"Elda..." Rubella drifted off. Warren stared at her for a moment more before huffing in amusement. Even though they had run as far from home as possible, Rubella still insisted on keeping in contact with that damn elf. Well, he would let her do as she pleased; she would do it regardless.

"How is she?" Foster asked a few minutes later when Warren once again joined the rest of the men down in the galley.

"Out like a light, and she should stay that way until morning," Warren replied. He stared at the sea-roughened wood in front of him for a moment before heaving a great sigh.

"She wants to send a letter to Elda, most likely before we leave," he finally admitted. He grimaced slightly in the face of Foster's scowl. He knew that Foster did not care for Elda or her husband.

"How pissed do you think she would be if I sailed off before she could get that letter out?" Foster asked as he toyed with a dagger.

"Enough that she would make sailing anywhere very difficult for you," Warren stated with a small smile. Rubella was in charge of getting them where they needed to go, her powers helped with that. As such, if Foster chose to sail without letting her mail her letter, she could make sure that they did not see land until almost all their stores were used up. Doing so would not only piss off Foster, but it would also bring down Nadia's wrath, and that was something that no one wanted. Before Foster could reply, Terrence the ship's cook came over.

"Anyone want to play cards?" he asked with a smirk. Everyone on the ship knew that Warren's favorite past time was cards, and that Foster could not stand by while others played if he was free.

"Pull up a bench, my good man. And prepare to lose some of your hard earned money," Warren stated quickly as he moved to make room for the other man on the bench.

"Oh no, tonight it will be you who loses their well-earned cash," Terrence replied with another smirk. Foster smiled slightly at their suddenly upbeat attitudes before he scowled again. While he enjoyed Elda and Atherton's visits, this was not the best time for them to come aboard. Though she was always the one who let them know when they were in port, Rubella hated both people deeply. No one but Warren knew why, and after she had created a hurricane in her anger, no one asked why. Sighing quietly as he acknowledged that this was a battle he was not going to win, Foster turned his attention back to the card game. It was time to earn a little more money.

Chapter 6

Rayne looked around her small cage and once again snarled at the man walking toward her with a tray. She knew that she had to eat something, but her anger was still so high she could barely open her mouth without screaming in fury.

"You must eat something, miss," the man stated softly. In truth, Rayne liked this sailor. He was kinder than any of the others who'd made lewd comments at her.

"I find it hard to eat in such a disgraceful manner. Never have I been treated thusly," Rayne muttered as she spit to one side in disgust. Even if she was nobility, she could still show her hatred. The state in which she referred was to the chains that held her bound to her cage. The sailors had been warned of her powers and had taken precautions. She could not bend metal to her will, the particles of Earth that made up the metal were too small for her to mold.

"I will feed you if you allow me, miss," the sailor stated as he nodded to her guards. They exchanged a look before opening her cell door. The sailor stepped in bearing a laden tray. Looking at the soup and bread presented to her, Rayne felt her mouth start to water.

"Fine, but I want you to taste it first," Rayne consented.

"Don't trust me?" the man asked with a small smirk.

"I would be foolish to trust the people that had me thrust up like a pig and shipped off to the Americas like some common slave," Rayne hissed in anger. The sailor stared at her for a moment before setting the plate down close to her.

"True enough," he stated. Keeping his eyes locked with her own, he slowly raised the spoon of soup to his mouth. Rayne watched intently as he tasted both her soup and bread. He even took a generous helping of the pudding that had come with him. Rayne couldn't help the small smile that showed with that motion.

"I think it is safe," he whispered as if they were sharing a secret.

"Do you have another spoon?" Rayne asked just as quietly. Now the sailor's face twisted with confusion.

"No, why?"

"Indirect kisses," Rayne whispered again. She watched as a dull red raced across his features before another smirk returned. She laughed.

"You sure are cheeky for a prisoner," he stated, holding the spoon out for her. Rayne allowed spoon after spoon of the sweet and spicy soup to cross her lips without comment. As she ate, she took a closer look at this man. His arms were strongly built--*A deck worker*, she thought--and his hair looked like it was blond once but had since been darkened by the sun. He had a strong brow and lips that looked like they smiled often.

"It is impolite to stare, miss," the sailor stated after many moments of silence. Rayne thought of being embarrassed for only a moment before shrugging it off. She had nowhere to go, and didn't know what these sailors had been told to do with her once they reached land. For all she knew, she was to be sold off or worse, so she would allow herself this one selfish pleasure.

"I only stare because I enjoy what I am seeing," she replied with as much of a shrug as she could accomplish in the chains.

"Indeed," was his only reply. After another moment, she finished and the sailor picked up the leftovers.

"What is your name?" Rayne called out to him. He paused at the cell door and replied, "My name is Kinta, miss." Without waiting for a reply he swiftly left the way he had come.

"Kinta, huh? Interesting man," Rayne stated to herself. Belly full for the first time in four days, Rayne allowed herself to drop into a peaceful sleep.

~~~

After the girls had calmed down, Kaywinnet convinced them that it was time to get some sleep. She promised them that they would talk more about their powers in the morning, and also cautioned them.

"You guys shouldn't use your abilities again until we can get you proper teachers. Using your abilities without the proper training can cause you to burn out, so to speak," she said as she stood in the middle of their room. The girls were settled in their beds and stared at her with wide eyes. Kaywinnet wanted to chuckle; even though they were both seventeen, they looked at her with the awe of toddlers.

"What do you mean *burn out?*" Sarafina asked.

"I mean it literally in your case, and figuratively in yours, Rhoswen. To burn out means to use up your abilities, and yes it can be done. When you have no training, simple things such as lighting a match, take up more of your energy. Burning up simply means becoming too tired to be of any use," Kaywinnet explained.

"And that is really bad?" Rhoswen asked.

"It can be. Usually all a person needs to do is rest after they burn out, but for people like Sarafina whose natural affinity is towards fire, it can be very dangerous. If you were to burn out to a severe degree, it is possible for you to die."

"DIE!" Sarafina gasped. Her eyes grew huge.

"I didn't mean to frighten you, I just felt like I had to explain," Kaywinnet sighed as she realized that she was going to have to explain fully before either girl would settle for the night.

"Our abilities come from the Mother, or Nature I suppose you could say. But there is more to it than that. They are not only a part of us, they make up our cores. Rhoswen, your core flows like a gentle stream, while yours burns like the hottest sun Sarafina. Your parents and I all have earth affinities, and so our cores are settled and unmoving like the earth. There are others whose cores are so light that their spirits fly on the wind. To burn out is to diminish our core. It is as if whichever element is our opposite finds its way into our cores and smothers them. For everyone besides fire, our cores are very hard to fully extinguish. You cannot get rid of air. Water may evaporate but still remains water as steam. The earth is solid and takes many years to blow or wash away, and though it may burn, it simply becomes a new form of earth. Fire can be fully extinguished with water. *Wet wood is hard to burn*, is the saying amongst our people. When your parents find out what your affinity is Sarafina, you will be put under strict training. The danger of you burning out far outshines your sister's," Kaywinnet explained softly but firmly. She stared at the girls for a few moments as silence filled the room. Sighing, she stood from her seated position on the edge of Sarafina's bed and moved to the door.

"I will see you both in the morning."

"Goodnight," the twins called as the door closed behind her. As soon as the door shut, Rhoswen made her way over to her sister.

"Don't worry, I'll help you. Just like I did today," she whispered, gathering her sister close. Kaywinnet had not seen Sarafina start to shake as she explained about their cores.

"Do you think they will separate us--I mean for training?" Sarafina asked. Rhoswen knew that the answer was yes--after all, she would hardly benefit from fire training--but she knew what her sister needed to hear.

"They can try," she stated firmly, holding Sarafina tightly.

Chapter 7

Nadia woke up with a blistering headache and a scowl. She hated losing to Rubella when they had drinking competitions. Especially since she was by far the better drinker, but as always, Rubella had cheated. She had gotten Nadia to drink faster than usual-- and as a result, between the two of them, Nadia was the drunker one in the end. And though it had seemed as if she had won, or so she had proclaimed the night before, the blistering headache showed the true winner of last night's battle.

"Alright, darling?" Foster asked from the doorway with a grin. He had watched his wife wake up and scowl at the dresser. It seemed to be a habit of hers when she woke up hung over. He could only guess what the poor thing had done to displease her.

"Stop grinning," Nadia growled.

"How do you know I'm grinning? You aren't even looking over here," Foster asked, his grin growing.

"Because, love, you are always grinning, more so when I am hung over. You think it is hilarious."

"Well I did warn you not to let Rubella drink you under the table again. Although I think you were doing better than her, considering that you actually made it to your bed last night without help."

Nadia looked toward her husband at that, a small smile creeping across her face.

"I did leave her on the dock didn't I?"

"Yes, Captain. Warren had to fetch her and put her to bed," Foster responded. He took a moment to consider his next words before figuring that now was just as good as later.

"She is going to be writing to Elda."

Nadia's frown came back. It wasn't that she disliked Elda and Atherton, it was just that Rubella disliked them. And when Rubella was unhappy, they had a hard time at sea.

"Has she done so yet?" Nadia asked swinging her feet out of bed.

"To my knowledge she is still asleep," Foster replied. He watched silently as Nadia quickly--well, as quickly as a hung over person could move--put on her clothes for the day.

"I'll go talk to her then. Have we got another shipment yet?" she asked, jumping right back into captain mode.

"Aye, picked one up this morning. Ol' Joe at the pub sent one our way earlier. Apparently you did get to askin' him about another job before you got lost in your tankard," Foster replied.

"Good, I'll go see if I can talk Rubella out of sending off a letter to people she despises. If not, we will send it before we leave. This time, however, I will not be waiting around until they show up. After we drop off this shipment, we have to head to the Americas," Nadia said gruffly as she pulled on her boots.

"Why the Americas?" Foster enquired.

"I have to see my sister," Nadia replied. She smiled at the sight of Foster's grimace.

"Oh, come now. She isn't that bad."

"Last time we saw her she claimed I had made a pact with the devil and tried to burn me," Foster replied dryly. Nadia laughed at the memory and strolled over to where he stood in the doorway.

"She was only joking," Nadia stated rising on her toes a bit to receive a kiss. Foster kissed her softly before pulling away.

"If she does it again, I'll feed her to the alligator that lives in her swamp," he stated before walking away, Nadia's laugher drifting after him.

~~~

Hine paced back in forth in his lounge muttering under his breath. He was a very influential man. He had a hand in almost every major government agency in Great Britain. Hine had no weaknesses when it came to the iron hand he used to control his vast network of spies and supporters. In a way, he was as important to the economy and well-being of the British people as the Queen of England herself. Or so he allowed himself to believe. He did, however, have one weakness that would cripple him in an instant. A son named Adrian. It was this son that had him pacing and muttering to himself now.

"Send him in," he finally bade to his manservant. The man nodded and turned sharply toward the door. Not even a minute later his son strode through the door, head held high. Adrian was a tall muscular boy with large hazel eyes and an ever-present grin. The grin was missing at this moment because he knew he was in trouble. Stopping to stand before his father, Adrian allowed his shoulder length hair to cover his face.

"You know, I thought I raised an intelligent son," Hine stated after a moment of looking at his apparently contrary offspring. Adrian's shoulders hunched a little at the barb, but still he said nothing.

"I thought I raised a son who knew that what was off-limits was off-limits for a reason. That some places shouldn't be ventured into, and that some things should. Not. Be. Touched!" Hine hissed as he drew close to his son.

"Father, I…"

"Silence!" Hine cut him off. He was furious not because his son had disobeyed him, but because Adrian could have been seriously injured in his stupidity. As it was, he had been hurt.

"Show me your arm," Hine stated calmly. Adrian searched his face for a moment before lifting his right arm up and offering it to his father.

Hine held it softly, and slowly pushed up the fabric of his son's silken cream-colored button-down. Adrian hissed a bit as the shirt caught on the raw skin underneath. Hine hissed as well as he took in the large burn that covered his son's forearm.

"Why haven't you treated this yet?" Hine asked calmly. He gently tugged his son over to his desk where he kept a spare medical kit. There had been times where his spies had needed a bit of fixing up before they could tell him their reports.

"Nana said that it would do me good to let it sting for a bit. She said that it would teach me to leave well enough alone," Adrian mumbled. He hissed again as his father dabbed the burn with burn salve.

"And have you learned your lesson?" Hine asked, his head bent over his task. It was not a terrible burn, but he imagined it stung quite a bit left out to the elements as it was.

"Yes, sir."

"You shouldn't lie to your father," Hine stated dryly. He didn't need to look up to see Adrian's smile. The boy had been getting into mischief since he was seven years old. Any forbidden place in the manor was eventually explored. Every booby trap was flipped and every trap was sprung until Adrian knew almost all of his father's secrets.

"I am sorry, father. I should have been more careful," Adrian replied. He winced as his father tied off the bandage.

"There are certain things that are going to be happening here that I don't want you to be around for. Because of this, and your propensity to get into things that you shouldn't," here Hine paused to send his son a pointed look, "I want you to go with Nadia and her crew to the Americas."

"You can't be serious!" Adrian exclaimed.

"It is 'cannot,' and I am entirely serious," Hine replied. Adrian scowled at his father, upset both at the correction of his grammar and the fact that he was being sent away.

"For how long this time?" Adrian asked.

"Oh, do not look at me like that. You love to visit Nadia, so do not pretend you are upset. As of right now I am not sure how long you will be gone. It depends on how long Nadia plans to be visiting Kamali."

"I hate aunt Kamali," Adrian muttered.

"If you don't annoy her, she won't turn you into a newt again," Hine stated calmly. Adrian's scowl deepened before he stomped to the door.

"Is that all?" he snapped. Hine raised an eyebrow at his tone. Adrian sighed and attempted to rein in his temper.

"I am sorry, Father. Was there anything else?" Adrian asked again once he had calmed down.

"No, Son. Go pack for a long trip. I will accompany you to Nadia's ship. There are some things I must talk to her about," Hine stated as he waved his son away. Leaning against the side of his desk for a few moments after Adrian's departure, Hine finally turned his attention to other matters. It was time to find a replacement for Rayne.

~~~

Sarafina and Rhoswen stood before their parents, a heavy tension permeating the air. Kaywinnet had convinced them to inform their parents about their newly developed abilities. Rhoswen was less nervous than Sarafina, who was practically cowering behind her sister.

"We have come to tell you that we know about our inheritance," Rhoswen began after her parents had settled down. Gama and Hilt shared a look before turning their attention back to their daughters.

"And which part of your inheritance is that?" Gama asked not wanting to tip the girls off about their nymph lineage if they didn't already know.

"It would be easier if we just showed you," Rhoswen replied. Turning to Sarafina she whispered in her ear.

"Don't get too mad, but think about the fact that they have been keeping this a secret from us for years."

Sarafina's eyes sparked and she stepped forward. Staring straight at her parents she snapped. Upon snapping, a small flame appeared on her index finger. She maintained eye contact with her parents not noticing that the flame was slowly growing.

"Calm down, Sara," Rhoswen's voice came through her sister's angry haze. Breaking eye contact with her parents, Sarafina glanced at her hand that was now inflamed. Knowing that if she started to panic it would simply continue to grow, she took short breaths. The flame remained stationary, but it did not extinguish. Seeing this for the opportunity that it was, Rhoswen stepped toward her sister. Remembering what it felt like the last time she came to Sarafina's rescue, Rhoswen willed water to encase both of her hands. When she was sure that both hands were fully covered, she gently encased Sarafina's glowing hand.

"Thank you," Sarafina whispered as she watched Rhoswen put out her hand in the same way she had put out her arm the night before. Grinning at her, Rhoswen simply turned to look at their parents. Gama and Hilt sat silently observing. Their eyes had grown wide when they saw the flames erupt in Sarafina's hand, and wider still as they witnessed the control Rhoswen already had over her own power.

"So do you have something that you want to tell us?" Sarafina asked. Her voice held just a note of scorn that had Gama frowning at her daughter.

"What would have been the point of telling you about this before your abilities had manifested, Sarafina?" Gama asked. "There was the possibility that you would not have had any abilities at all. It has been known to skip generations the more diluted our species becomes."

Sarafina chose not to answer knowing that her mother was making a valid point. Instead she simply pouted.

"You will need tutors," Hilt stated after a moment of silence. Rhoswen nodded while Sarafina simply continued to ignore the room at-large.

"Of course they will have to be different tutors. There is no one that we know of that contains both the fire and water affinities. They cancel each other out. There is also the matter of where Sarafina is going to train," Gama put in as she studied her children.

"What do you mean *where*?' Sarafina finally spoke up. She shared a slightly scared look with Rhoswen who simply grabbed and squeezed her hand in reassurance.

"Well, we can't have you train in the backyard where Rhoswen will be, you will burn down all the trees. Also it would be dangerous for you to train together. Your abilities being what they are, you would simply continuously cancel each other out. Rhoswen you will be tutored in the backyard, and Sarafina you will be tutored in the basement," Hilt replied.

"We don't want to be separated," Rhoswen hastily cut in before Sarafina could reply. She saw the look on her sister's face. She looked terrified.

Gama saw the look as well and she frowned in concern. What had happened when the girls discovered their abilities to have Sarafina looking so frightened?

"It cannot be helped," was all that Hilt would say. Knowing that there was nothing that she could do, Rhoswen nodded to her parents before pulling Sarafina from the room. Gama and Hilt observed them immediately begin to argue as they left. Sarafina looked very distraught while Rhoswen's face, though determined, looked a bit strained as well.

"What do you think happened?" Gama asked quietly.

"I'm not sure, but we should keep an eye on them. Sarafina especially, she seems unusually upset about being separated from Rhoswen," Hilt replied. One hand came up to gently stroke his chin as he went over all the details of their conversation again in his head.

"Do you think we should ask Kaywinnet to come back for their first session?" Gama asked. She seemed reluctant, as the girl had only just returned to her home.

"If it would make the girls feel more secure then I think that would be a good idea. We shall call upon her later today," Hilt finally replied. With that said, he stood and began to leave the room.

"Where are you going?" Gama asked.

Turning back to his wife, Hilt observed her for a few moments before sighing. "I am going to get into contact with some of my contacts. I want to know if anyone knows where Rayne has disappeared to, and find out if any of them are willing to teach the girls."

"You mean I may get to meet one of your elusive contacts?" Gama stated in feigned shock. Hilt laughed at her tone.

"You just might. I think I have two in mind that would work perfectly for our needs. It just depends on if they are available." With that said, he continued on his way. Gama chose to stay in the living room as her family dispersed. Still a bit shaken by Sarafina's response to being separated from her sister, she pulled out her pack of cigarettes. It was at times like this that she wished she hadn't given up drinking.

Chapter 8

Rayne had finally gotten the metal to do what she wanted. That meant that she had rubbed her wrist so raw that the blood had finally acted as a sufficient lubricant to slide her wrist out. She kept her hands behind her back, unwilling to give herself away just yet. Kinta, the sailor from before, had come back a couple more times to feed her as the days had passed. She assumed that they thought that he was the only one that she would eat from. In a way they were right; she didn't trust any of them, and this sailor was simply more tolerable than any of the others. She had no idea how long they had been traveling, or how close they were to the Americas.

"Hello, miss," she heard from outside her cell. Stiffening she lifted her head to lock eyes with the captain. The man was very tall and very broad. She disliked him immensely, even though he had been very nice to her the entire trip. It was simply his size that scared her. If she were to make an escape she would have to get passed this man.

"Captain," she stated simply, nodding in acknowledgement. Besides Kinta, this man was the only other person on this Mother forsaken boat that she could tolerate.

"I am to inform you that we will be reaching land within the next day. There we are to deliver you to a man named Pit. After that, we are to turn around and not think about you again," the captain stated gruffly. His voice sounded like he was talking with gravel in his mouth.

"I see."

The captain then started to laugh causing Rayne to jerk in surprise.

"You see nothing, young lady. I'm not sure what you did to annoy our payer so badly, but once you leave shore you are mine to deal with. And I do not sell young women to slavers."

Rayne's eyes widened as she discovered what was to be done with her. Slavers were very sick men, and if she knew Thena, this Pit would know to keep her chained or risk her using her abilities on him to escape.

"So what do you plan to do with me?" Rayne finally asked.

"Well, considering you already have one hand free, and I have finally found the little worm that was reporting on you," here the captain stopped to laugh at the shock on Rayne's face before continuing, "I figure I would let you out of the cage and give you a few choices." After saying this the captain motioned to one of the men who had come with him to unlock the cage door. Rayne stiffened again and watched with apprehension as he entered, a ring of keys dangling from his hand.

"Want to give me the hand that is still in the manacle?" he asked, a broad smile stuck on his face. After a moment of staring at him, Rayne started to smile as she offered him her still trapped hand. He quickly unlocked it and moved on to her ankles. Once she was free he offered a hand to help her up.

"So what are my choices?" Rayne asked as she cradled her bleeding hand.

"How about we get you fixed up and fed first. Then we will talk." With that said, the captain turned and left the cell. Rayne only hesitated for a moment before following him out. She followed his broad back as he walked up the stairs. Rayne raised a hand to help her see when she was suddenly hit with sunlight.

"Ah, it has been nearly two weeks since you were put down there. You'll be fine in a moment," the captain called back to her. Rayne could only nod though she was sure that he didn't see her. The captain finally ducked into a room and waited for her to enter. Entering the room she let out a small laugh.

"I thought you were a ship hand," she stated softly. At her words, Kinta turned from the table where he had been setting up his medical supplies.

"We don't have a full crew this trip. Some of us have to do more than one job," he explained as she came closer.

"And which is your normal job, ship hand or medic?" Rayne asked, allowing him to examine her hurt wrist.

"I'm a medic who enjoys climbing the rigging every once and a while," Kinta responded. He led her over to the table and patted it, indicating that she should jump up. Rayne did so and winced as her muscles protested. She hadn't been allowed to stand for the last two weeks, and her legs were protesting all of the sudden motions.

"I can give you a mixture to help your muscles regain some strength in them, but I warn you it tastes foul. This is going to hurt," Kinta stated just before he started to dab her wrist with some type of mixture. Rayne hissed as the broken skin on her wrist started to burn, but she resisted the need to pull her arm away. She watched as he dabbed her whole wrist with the mixture before taking some cloth in hand. He began to wrap her wrist and Rayne hissed again.

"Too tight?" he asked, pausing.

"A bit, but," Rayne rolled the wrist in question a bit, "I should be fine." Kinta nodded as he continued to wrap her wrist. As this happened, the captain simply stood to the side and observed. He had known that Kinta was the only person that Rayne would accept food from, and thus he was going to be in charge of her for the remainder of the time that she would be on board.

"Alright captain, she is as good as she is going to be. She needs food and water though," Kinta stated as he stepped back and began to clean up his medical area.

"Alright then miss if you would follow me."

"Rayne."

"Excuse me?" the captain turned to look at his reluctant charge.

"My name is Rayne. Since I'm not a prisoner anymore, you might as well use it," Rayne stated.

"I always said you were far too cheeky for a prisoner," Kinta said from behind her. The captain snorted before beckoning Rayne to follow him. After glancing once more at the medic, Rayne followed the captain out. She followed silently as he ducked into another room.

"Have a seat," the captain said as he pointed out a vacant bench to her. Rayne realized that they were in the galley, and most of the other crewmembers were eating. Most of the talking had stopped when she had entered, but as she took a seat the men continued their conversations. After a moment of looking around, Rayne turned back to the captain to see that he had placed a plate of food in front of her.

"Eat up, lass. I will tell you your options as you eat. Doctor's orders and all." Rayne grinned at him as she dug in; she was enjoying the ability to eat with her own hands for the first time in weeks.

"So here are my suggestions to you: either you can stay aboard my ship and become one of my crew. We would have to change your appearance a bit, but we would manage. Or I can leave you with a friend of mine on the Americas. She has a sister that visits every so often that owns a ship. That sister can bring you back to England the next time she travels that way. Either way I cannot bring you back the way you are, I like my head where it is," the captain informed her as he watched her eat. Rayne paused for a moment contemplating her options.

"Is it possible for me to do both? We will be on the Americas soon. You can enquire with your friend when her sister will be arriving next. When you find that out I could stay with you until that time," Rayne suggested. Now that she knew the crew had no inclination to hurt her, she wanted to experience more of the world. Ever since she had entered the Fold she had been kept under close surveillance because of her abilities. She wanted to see more of the world, and working on a ship would be the easiest way to do that.

"There is the chance that we could miss her. I never know how long a voyage is going to last. From where we are now it will take another two months to make it to my friends. We are on the wrong side of the Americas as it is. We are at the whims of the sea and the wind," the captain responded. He stroked his chin as he thought over her proposal. He liked the lass; she had spunk, and would make a fine addition to his crew. He was a man of equal opportunity and had many other women working on his ship, so he was not worried for her.

"I can help you there, but I really want to see the world. I am not so eager to head back to England. I mean the people that sent me to the Americas are still there. I don't think I'm very safe until I can get some of my friends in on what has happened to me. That doesn't mean that I don't want to go back. No one sells me!" Rayne stated as she finished up the rest of her food. Pushing the plate to one side she folded her hands in front of her to wait for the captain's decision.

"Alright you can stay on. We will go talk to my friend once we get to her dock and make a more concrete plan then. How can you help us combat nature?"

"Let me show you," Rayne stated with a smug smile. She would prove her worth, even if it meant exposing her abilities to people outside the Fold.

~~~

Sarafina tried not to hyperventilate as she stood across from the man who was to be her tutor. He was an imposing figure to be sure. Taller than her by at least a head and with wide shoulders that seemed to take up all the space in the room, his shoulder length black hair was combed back to show off his impressive forehead and sharp jaw line. He said his name was Walt.

"Alright, Miss Sarafina shall we begin?" Walt's gruff voice cut through her inner panic. She swallowed and nodded to show her readiness.

"I want you to concentrate on your inner fire. Think about the emotions that you associate with it when you manifest. What is that emotion?"

"Anger, or embarrassment," Sarafina responded.

"WRONG!" Walt snapped at her causing her to jump.

"What do you mean wrong? You asked me what emotions I felt when I manifested my fire. That's how I felt," Sarafina snapped after she had recovered from her shock.

"And I am telling you that those emotions are wrong. You should never associate fire with such volatile emotions. You run the risk of burning out before you learn how to control yourself. No, the emotions that you should associate with it are happiness, safety, and love," Walt explained.

"Why those three?" Sarafina asked, still feeling frustrated. She tried to remain calm and listen to her teacher, but the longer she was away from Rhoswen the more upset she became. They had fought their separation so violently that their parents had questioned them heavily. After finding out exactly how the girls had discovered their abilities, Gama and Hilt were even more insistent on getting them tutors. They didn't seem to understand that Sarafina was afraid of her abilities, and only felt calm when Rhoswen was near.

"When you sit by the fire with a book how do you feel?" Walt asked as he paced towards her. He observed his pupil with a sharp eye. She was stiff as a board and he could see that she was already frustrated.

"I feel happy and calm," Sarafina replied.

"I see, and if you could cover yourself in fire knowing that you wouldn't be burned when you were in danger how would you feel?"

"I suppose I would feel safe," Sarafina answered, her face clearing as she started to understand.

"Correct, and finally when you love someone doesn't that love burn within you like a fire?" Walt asked with a smile. Sarafina grinned back.

"Yes, yes it does."

"This is why these emotions will help you manifest your fire without it getting away from you. Anger, embarrassment, fear, these things will cause your fire to misbehave."

"Misbehave?" Sarafina questioned.

"When you have manifested in the past, have you been able to control the fire? Keep it exactly where you want it without it running away from you so to speak?" Sarafina's face blanched as she remembered the fire racing up her arm as she began to panic.

"Yes, I see your point," Sarafina whispered. Walt observed her pensive face for a moment as he determined whether or not he should ask her what caused such a strained look.

"So what do I do first?" Sarafina asked.

"First, you concentrate on one of the three emotions I talked about before. After you have found an emotion you have the most connection with, I want you to allow it to fill you up. When you tell me that you are full, then I will prompt you to manifest. Now concentrate, you may sit if it makes it easier for you," Walt explained.

Sarafina nodded in understanding and chose to remain standing as she closed her eyes. Thinking back to when she would sit in the living room in front of the fire while Rhoswen washed dishes in the background, Sarafina allowed the happiness to consume her. When she was sure that she couldn't get any happier she stated, "I'm ready."

"Alright, I want you to manifest fire into your right hand. Only your right hand," Walt commanded as he watched her closely.

Sarafina willed the fire in her soul to come to the surface revolving around her right hand. When she was sure she had it, she opened both her right hand and eyes. Sitting on her palm was a tiny ball of fire.

"I did it!" Sarafina breathed in astonishment. Walt nodded in approval.

"Now make it bigger, but still contain it to your right hand," Walt prompted.

"Alright," Sarafina stated. She began to focus again, willing the flame to grow larger; however, this time it did not work. Sarafina concentrated harder, pulling on the feeling that had allowed her to pull the fire so easily to the surface. It was not to be.

"Damn it," Sarafina muttered, as the flame remained small. She did not notice that the beautiful orange color had started to turn white where the flames met her palm. Walt noticed and grew worried.

"Calm down, Sarafina. Frustration will only cause your fire to burn hotter. The hotter you burn, the more dangerous you become. Calm down!" Walt commanded.

"Do NOT tell me to calm down!" Sarafina snarled. Her eyes snapped open and Walt took a step back. Her pupils were red and the fire in her palm enlarged to encompass her entire hand. Instead of taking enjoyment in her accomplishment, Sarafina's frustration grew even more.

"Why can't I get this right when I'm not using anger?" Sarafina cried in her mind. She became consumed with her anger and the fire that started in her palm started to travel up her arm.

"Sarafina!" Walt cried. He moved forward to shake her out of her trance, but had to step back when her fire suddenly lashed out at him.

"Dear Mother!" he cursed as the fire grew hotter and covered more of her body. Remarkably her clothing was fine, as if a layer stood between her and the inferno she was producing. Walt looked around and hoped that the cement basement they were in would hold up against the heat. His attention was suddenly drawn back to Sarafina when she let out a scream. Fearful that she had begun to burn, Walt turned back to her, only to drop to the floor. Sarafina had opened her arms and screamed out her frustrations, the fire shooting away from her body in all directions. When Walt looked up, everything was charred, the ceiling was on fire, and Sarafina was nowhere to be seen.

~~~

"Very good, very good," Mathias stated softly as he observed Rhoswen control a large ball of water. She had produced it easily enough, and already had a great mastery of her abilities. Rhoswen laughed as she watched the ball of water bounce and dance as she willed it. He had asked her to think of the emotions that caused her to produce water. Mathias was only slightly surprised when she had told him that when she had first manifested the water she had been thinking of protection. It was an odd feeling to associate with a water element; most people used calmness, or serenity. Mathias smiled a bit as he observed her joyful expression as she manipulated the water.

"You are a natural. There is very little…" Mathias was cut off by a loud boom coming from the house.

"What in the world?" Mathias muttered. He turned to look at Rhoswen only to see the ball of water crash to the ground. Rhoswen's face had turned ashen, and she only stood still for a moment before taking off at a full on sprint. Mathias only caught her whispered word as she flew by him.

"Sarafina…"

Rhoswen crashed into the living room just as Sarafina did from the other side. Rhoswen could only stare at her sister in shock. Her clothing was burnt and her face blackened with soot. The most terrifying thing was that her hair was on fire, glowing around her face like a demonic halo.

"Sara," Rhoswen whispered as she immediately called up a bubble of water. Taking hesitant steps toward her sister who simply stood there with wide eyes, Rhoswen gently set the bubble of water onto her head. Steam immediately erupted throughout the room and soon Sarafina's cries could be heard.

"I couldn't do it, I couldn't. It just got hotter, and bigger, and then it was too much. And oh, Wen, I think I set the house on fire," Sarafina cried as she desperately clung to her sister.

"Hush now, hush. We will fix this, mother and father will fix this," Rhoswen tried to calm her sister down. At her words Sarafina jerked out of her embrace.

"NO! They have done enough. I can't do this. I can't!" Sarafina screamed. Without waiting for a reply Sarafina spun around and charged out the back door.

"SARA!" Rhoswen called out to her. She chased after her only to see her disappear into the forest at the edge of their grounds.

"Rhoswen, what has happened?" Kaywinnet called out from behind her. She had just arrived to find that Sarafina had apparently blown up the basement during her first lesson.

"Oh Kit, she's gone and I have to go after her," Rhoswen stated before running off as well.

"Wait!" Kaywinnet yelled as she raced to the open doorway. She saw Rhoswen disappear into the forest as her sister had done, and paused for a moment in indecision. She should go back and tell Gama and Hilt where the girls had gone, but there was no guarantee that the girls would come back. Especially if Sarafina thought that her parents would separate them again.

"Damn It!" Kaywinnet exclaimed in exasperation before she too ran off into the forest. She only hoped she would find them before something terrible happened to one of them.

Chapter 9

Kamali paced her living room, a small smile on her face. Everything was starting to come together, a little bit at a time.

"Soon everyone will be just where they are supposed to be. And then we will see who the real evil is. Isn't that right Chewy?" Kamali asked, as she paused to absently pat her pet on the head. Her pet happened to be a full-grown alligator, but that meant little to Kamali. Most would say that she was an eccentric woman, living in the middle of the bayou in the middle of New Orleans. Actually, most would call her a witch, which wasn't completely false.

"Witch, elf, nymph, what does it really matter?" Kamali asked Chewy as she passed him again. The gator said nothing, only watched his mistress as she paced. He was so large that although his head and upper body were situated quite nicely in her living room, his tail and lower body were still outside in the water some fifteen feet away from her front door.

"You are talking to yourself again, Kamali," a young voice spoke up from the other side of the room. Kamali paused for a moment to survey her newest guest but then resumed her pacing.

"I am not talking to myself. I am talking to Chewy."

"I see, and has Chewy ever responded?" the voice asked again, amusement lacing their voice. Kamali paused once more to share a look with her pet. Chewy seemed to smile, his mouth opening to show off his many rows of teeth.

"Only once, but it was a very important word," Kamali replied.

"Oh, and what word was that?" the voice called out again.

"Mother."

"Aww, that is cute," the voice cooed at the alligator that simply stared at the visitor.

"What are you doing here, Phina? You should still be on guard," Kamali asked her guest, as she finally came to a stop in front of her. The woman in her midst was tall and slender. Her youthful face gave many the impression that she was much younger than she actually was. Her almost ruby red eyes complemented her dark black hair. On her hip she wore a very long, very sharp sword. It extended behind her like a tail, the very edge of it just brushing along the ground as she walked.

"What, I can't take a break every once in a while? It's not like he is going anywhere," Phina scoffed as she leaned against the wall nearest to her. Kamali shot her a quelling look, causing her to sigh in defeat.

"Don't be angry with me. I'm there every day from morning till night; one hour away from him is not going to cause the end of the world," Phina argued quietly.

"You don't know that, it might," Kamali retorted quietly. She stood in the middle of her living room staring intently out the window. Beyond her house stood the marshes of New Orleans, a place that she had deemed acceptable to live in almost eight centuries ago. Back when this land was truly nothing but marshes, and the humans had yet to create a hub of enjoyment so close by.

"I'll get back to him then," Phina stated with a huff. She spun on her heel and was halfway out the door before Kamali called her back.

"We are going to be having a lot of visitors soon. I want you to be on your best behavior. The time is coming. He will wake up soon," Kamali calmly stated. Phina's eyes widened in shock as she sat down heavily in a nearby chair.

"What do you mean he will be waking up soon? What is different about this time as opposed to the last seven hundred years?" she asked quietly.

"Now all those who should be awake are awake, it is the perfect time. Also, his mother is close to passing, you should feel as much yourself," Kamali stated. Phina stared at her in confusion. She hated it when Kamali started to talk in riddles. She did pause for a moment to reach for the connection to someone she had forgotten about. The woman's energy was faint, but it still pulsed with light…just.

"I'll go back then, wouldn't want him to wake up by himself," Phina stated after a moment of silence, hauling herself to her feet. She was out the door before Kamali could comment.

"Things are about to get very interesting around here, Chewy. Better get ready…" Kamali's voice drifted off as she left the living room for some place further in the house. Chewy simply sat where his mistress had left him, a wide alligator-smile plastered across his face.

~~~

Sarafina stumbled through the forest blindly. The tears streaming down her face prevented almost all sight, but she didn't care. She was terrified of what she had done to their home. Even now she did not know if it was still standing, or if in her frustration she had burned it to the ground.

"Stupid, stupid, stupid girl," she cried out as she leaned against a tree. Shrieking in surprise Sarafina jumped away as the tree caught on fire. Instead of stopping to investigate, she simply took off running again. This repeated every time she stopped to take a breath.

"*I need to get out of the forest!*" Sarafina thought as she pushed ahead. She wasn't sure what lay on the other side of the large forest that surrounded their lands, only that there would be no people.

"*I'll go to the coast, and sail far away from here,*" Sarafina decided even as she dashed around fallen trees and ducked under low hanging branches. In her head she knew that she would be unable to leave, not without Rhoswen at least. Pausing once again to breathe heavily, she made sure that she kept away from the trees this time, Sarafina fought off the urge to cry.

"Sarafina!"

Jerking upright, Sarafina spun on her heel to look back the way she had come. She could have sworn she had heard Rhoswen's voice. As if thinking about her brought her into being, Rhoswen appeared a moment later between two trees.

"Oh thank the Mother. I was afraid I had lost you," Rhoswen stated as she quickly hurried over to her sister. Sarafina allowed her sister to wrap her up in a gentle embrace. Still, she fought the urge to cry.

"Sara, where are you going?" Rhoswen asked softly. She didn't want to set her sister off again, especially since she had just caught up with her.

"Away, away from here," Sarafina muttered into her sister's neck.

"Away where Sara? You can't keep running from your powers, they are a part of you. And if you don't learn to control them they could destroy you," Rhoswen urged her sister to see the logic in her statement. Pulling away slightly Sarafina looked into eyes so like her own.

"I'm going to the coast. I'm going to get on a boat and sail away from this place."

"You can't be serious!" Rhoswen exclaimed. Instead of answering, Sarafina merely stared at her. A number of protests jumped to the front of Rhoswen's mind, but as she studied her twin she took in the slight tremor that racked her body, the way that her breathing was still slightly frantic, and the look of terror and determination deep in her eyes. Rhoswen sighed deeply as she pushed away thoughts of other ways they could get away, like a plane or a car.

"Alright, but I'm coming with you," Rhoswen finally stated. Sarafina's face lit up and she swept her sister up into a crushing hug.

"You two aren't going anywhere without me!" a disjointed voice called out. Breaking apart, they looked around trying to find the source.

"Honestly, I leave for one day and you two cause chaos," Kaywinnet stated as she jumped down from the tree she was in to land before them. The girls traded looks of awe as they took in their friend's appearance. Kaywinnet had a bird sitting on her shoulder, a long whip held tightly in one hand, and a mighty frown on her face. Choosing to ignore the two for a moment, Kaywinnet turned to the bird and offered a hand to it. It nimbly hopped into her palm and she brought it around until she could see it properly.

"Thank you for the guidance, my friend. May the Mother bless you and your offspring," Kaywinnet spoke softly. The bird chirped in response and took flight. Taking another moment to shrink down her whip until it was once again in the shape of the bracelet that she always wore, Kaywinnet turned on her two friends with a mighty frown.

"Now, what in the world do you think you are doing running off like that?!" she snapped at the girls. Her voice caused both girls to snap to attention.

"I'm sorry," Sarafina muttered looking slightly ashamed.

"And so you should be," Kaywinnet agreed with a sharp nod. She stood for another moment contemplating the girls, and what she had overheard them saying.

"Well, if we are going to the coast, we had best be on our way."

"We?" Rhoswen asked as they once again began moving through the forest.

"Of course, you didn't really think that I would let you guys leave without me did you?" Kaywinnet asked with a smile.

Feeling much more at peace now that her sister and best friend were with her, Sarafina jumped onto Kaywinnet's back. "Thank you Kit!" she exclaimed.

Kaywinnet laughed at her renewed enthusiasm, gently returning the hug. "You are welcome, Sara," she replied with a smile.

~~~

"I am not dealing with this again, Rubella. It was your decision to contact them; if you didn't want to see them then you shouldn't have sent the message when everyone was asleep. You have no one to blame but yourself, and I will not have you taking your moods out on this ship. Now get out there and deal with it!" Nadia growled at her friend. Said friend was currently sulking in her cabin because Elda and Atherton had shown up that morning and refused to leave without seeing their old friend.

"It's only out of obligation that I tell them when we are in town. I don't want to see them, and they know this," Rubella muttered while glaring at the wall. She continued to pout until she felt the muzzle of a pistol against her head.

"I. Don't. Care," Nadia hissed. "Go out, talk to them for ten minutes, and get them off my ship so that we can leave."

Rubella sat for a moment more in shock before heaving a great sigh, it wasn't the first time Nadia had threatened to shoot her.

"Fine, I'll deal with it."

"Good, let me know how it goes. I'm going to the pub," with that Nadia holstered her gun and spun on her heel. Rubella waited until she knew she was gone before sticking her tongue out like a petulant child.

"Might as well get this over with," Rubella muttered. True, she hated Elda and Atherton, but it was a begrudging hatred. In truth, they were some of her oldest friends, but they reminded her of mistakes she had made in the past, mistakes that had lost her and Warren their homes and families. It was a past that she'd rather not remember; yet seeing Elda or Atherton always brought the memories back. It was enough to darken anyone's mood, and considering that Rubella's mood affected the weather, a dark mood was the last thing anyone on board wanted.

"There she is. We were beginning to think you were avoiding us," Elda stated happily as she noticed Rubella appear on deck. Her husband laughed quietly behind her. They both knew that they brought bad memories with them, but that didn't stop them from wanting to catch up with their oldest friend.

"Where is Warren?" Atherton asked as Rubella closed the distance between them.

"He is coming. One of the men hurt himself just before you arrived. Warren is currently patching him up," Rubella answered with a small smile. Before she could protest, Elda swept her up in a crushing hug.

"It is good to see you, hun. You must come home more often, we hardly see you anymore," Elda stated.

"I am at the whims of my captain, Elda. Where she goes I take her," Rubella replied in a slightly strangled voice.

"Honey, I think you may be killing her a bit," Atherton called to his wife quietly.

Seeing that Rubella was indeed turning a bit blue, Elda let go of her with a laugh.

"Sorry."

"It's fine," Rubella managed as she sucked in air.

"Trying to kill off my soul mate again Elda?" Warren asked as he topped the stairs to the deck, having just witnessed Elda release Rubella.

"Not on purpose. She is too fragile for her own good," Elda replied. They stared at each other for a moment before moving to hug one another in greeting.

"We will not stay long; I know how our visits distress you. We come with news from Hine," Elda stated quietly. Rubella and Warren crowded in closer to listen to the newest gossip.

Not long after that, Elda and Atherton took their leave. Rubella and Warren stood on deck watching them disappear down the dock.

"It looks like we are about to get a few more visitors," Rubella stated.

"Are we?" A voice asked from behind her. Turning her head, she smiled up into Foster's face.

"Oh yes," she replied with a positively cheeky grin.

"And who will be visiting this time?" Foster enquired, though he was pretty sure he knew who was coming. Rubella's face only looked like that for a few people after all.

"It looks like Adrian got into a bit of trouble again. Dear ol' daddy is planning on dropping him off soon. Looks like Nadia will have to put off leaving for just a little longer," Rubella stated clapping her hands in glee.

"Oh she will be so pleased," Foster stated sarcastically. He knew his wife would not be overjoyed with another delay, but he was looking forward to seeing Adrian again. The man had always had a soft spot for the boy, despite his penchant for mischief.

"I'm glad you think so, since you will be the one to tell her," Warren stated. Glancing at the man, Foster realized that while he had been lost in his own thoughts Rubella had taken that time to make her escape. Sighing, Foster resigned himself to informing his wife that they would once again be delayed.

Chapter 10

Rayne stood on the deck and stared out into the ocean. After a small demonstration where she caused the winds to blow faster and the water to become less choppy, she had been allowed to stay. Now working as a deckhand with some of the other females in the crew, Rayne could say that she felt at peace for the first time.

"We should be getting there pretty soon thanks to you," Kinta stated as he came to stand by her side. They had gotten on even better since Rayne was taken from her prison. Now only a few days from Kamali's island, Kinta was beginning to realize that he didn't want to see her go. Besides, the captain's friend Kamali was a bit strange and usually threatened to turn him into something.

"I live to please," Rayne replied quietly. She was a bit sad today. Sometime after being let out, she had asked for the date wanting to know how long she had been in the belly of the boat. It was hard to keep track of the days in the bottom of a ship, and she couldn't remember what day she had been shipped out. She had learned that it was February 24th. Today being the 28th of February, it was her best friend's birthday, and for the first time in remembrance she was missing it.

"What's the matter?" Kinta asked as he took in her drawn features. He would never admit it out loud, but she truly was beautiful. Her hair fell in braided curls down her back; her eyes were large and expressive, coupled with a sweet mouth that made him want to stare at her for hours. It was hard to keep his mind purely platonic; somehow he knew that she was not meant for him.

"I'm missing my friend's birthday for the first time in forever," Rayne replied with a sad sigh. She turned slightly to look at the man who had slowly become her friend. Months together on a ship at sea would do that to people. Rayne had not questioned why Thena would put her on a wooden vessel in this day and age, only concluding that the slower speed would keep her family from finding her. She did not begrudge the time that she had been given to get to know the crew, but she wondered how her parents were dealing with her disappearance.

"That must be tough. Were you guys close?"

"Like sisters, but closer. We did everything together when she was around. I had different duties than she did. My powers came a bit earlier and I needed more than one tutor. She had other friends, a pair of adorable twins that she hung out with when I was in lessons. But every other time we were together, and until now we have never missed a birthday." Rayne's voice shone with happiness and loneliness as she recounted her adventures with her friend.

"What is her name?" Kinta asked.

"Kaywinnet."

~~~

"Kaywinnet! Where in the world are we going?" Rhoswen asked as they walked toward a coastal town. It had taken them the better part of a day to get out of the forest, after that Kaywinnet had proclaimed that she knew exactly where to go and had proceeded to drag them straight to the coast. Rhoswen was pretty sure that she had gotten a good idea of where to go by talking to a few birds. It was still strange to know that she could do that.

"You said you wanted to go to the coast, so we are going to the coast. We can even board a ship once we get there, if we are so inclined. Although this town likes to pretend that it is still in the fourteenth century, so all of the ships are wooden," Kaywinnet paused to wince. She had never understood how an entire economy could work with such backwards thinking, however the town had been there for centuries. "This is the best place to go if you want to get away without your parents being able to track you: no credit cards, no passports, just cold hard cash works here," Kaywinnet responded as she navigated their little trio toward the town. Sarafina had become very quiet at the sight of the ocean.

"You alright, Sara?" Kaywinnet asked softly coming to a stop just outside of the town.

"I suppose…should I feel worried about that amount of water?" Sarafina asked. Her voice trembled a bit and she found herself disgusted at her own irrational fear. After all, her sister controlled water and she wasn't nearly as terrified of her.

"It isn't common, but it isn't unusual either for fire nymphs to avoid large amounts of water. Although if you fall in nothing will happen to you, I suppose it is simply an internal defense mechanism," Kaywinnet explained as she studied Sarafina's slightly ashen features. Her heart going out to the girl, she quickly gathered her up into a fierce hug.

"Do you want to just find a hotel to stay in for the night?" she asked softly into Sarafina's hair. After a moment Sarafina shook her head.

"I want to find a ship…I want to leave England. Get as far away from all this as I can," Sarafina whispered. She felt Kaywinnet sigh and resisted the urge to wince. She knew that she was being irrational and that her parents would worry, but she felt like she couldn't stay there any longer. Something out there was pulling at her core, and after studying her sister, she knew that Rhoswen had felt the pull too.

"Alright then, let's find us a ship," Kaywinnet replied pulling back to smile at both girls. Before she could take a step, however, Rhoswen called attention to something they had all overlooked.

"Kit, we didn't bring any money with us. How are we supposed to board a ship without paying?"

"Well, we can always offer to work for our passage… but lucky us, I did not run out of my house without money," Kaywinnet stated with a smile. Placing two fingers into her mouth she blew three long shrill whistles. The trio stood waiting for a moment before Kaywinnet's face broke into a large smile.

"There he is!" she stated laughing. Before either girl could question her, she raised an arm high above her head to allow a very large Eurasian sparrowhawk to land on her forearm.

"Mother abound! He is huge!" Sarafina exclaimed as she took in the bird on Kaywinnet's arm.

"Why is he so large? Sparrowhawks only get to be about forty-one centimeters long and that is only with the females. This one is obviously male, and he must be something like eighty-one centimeters long, almost twice the size of the largest female. Kit what have you been feeding him?" Rhoswen exclaimed as she too studied the animal. As the girls exclaimed over his size, the bird had dropped a medium sized pouch into Kaywinnet's hand.

"This is Albert, and I've had him since he was an egg. As to what I did to him, well let's just say he is my familiar of sorts. Most woodland nymphs have an animal guide, usually to help them hunt. Albert was given to me as an egg to raise, and because of my own powers, he is twice as big as he should be, twice as fast, twice as strong, and twice as sweet," Kaywinnet explained as she gently stroked the bird's belly. He had been following her since she entered the forest.

"What is he doing here?" Sarafina asked as she edged closer to the large bird. As she neared, his head swiveled around and he looked straight into her eyes. Sarafina gulped.

"Twice as sweet right?" she asked nervously as he continued to stare at her. Kaywinnet laughed softly.

"I called him. He brings things to me that I forget, or that I give him to hold on to. You both don't realize it but he comes with me everywhere. When I come over to your house he usually just hangs out in the forest. I left in such a rush today that I called him after I entered the forest to hold onto some of my things while I chased you," Kaywinnet explained. As the girls processed this new information, she gently tapped Albert's beak.

"Thank you, but go ahead and bring me the rest please. Wherever you hid it, just bring it here. And then we need to talk," she ordered once she had his attention. Albert stared at her for a moment before gently tugging on a lock of her hair, his way of agreeing to do as she asked. Kaywinnet smiled as she allowed him to launch himself back into the air. She grimaced slightly as his claws scraped her upon flight.

"Are you alright?" Rhoswen asked.

"Yeah, he is just peeved with me," Kaywinnet laughed as she inspected the very shallow cuts on her arm. If Albert had been truly mad he would have gouged her deeper.

"Why is he mad?" Sarafina asked, her attention still on the sky in the direction Albert had flown.

"I interrupted his meal. He hates carrying my backpack which is what I just asked him to get, and he hates large expanses of water with no trees," Kaywinnet replied with a small grin. Albert knew that if they were by the coast that they wouldn't be staying on land for much longer. He wasn't equipped to hunt for fish and after they got far enough away from land he wouldn't be able to hunt other birds. Albert had never been overly fond of human food.

Both girls nodded in understanding and the trio lapsed into silence as they awaited Albert's return. After ten minutes he showed up again, although this time he merely dropped Kaywinnet's backpack into her hands before flying up into the nearest tree. In his mouth was a small bird that he had obviously been eating. Deciding to give him a few moments to finish his meal Kaywinnet dug through her bag to find her wallet.

"I have £600, which should be enough to get us passage on something. And if that fails, it can be a deposit and we can work for the rest of the journey. Now girls, there is something very important we have to talk about," Kaywinnet stated seriously.

"Alright," Sarafina replied, suddenly feeling apprehensive.

"I understand that there was a bit of a failure back at the house, but Sara you can't go without a tutor. You'll burn out too fast. Your temper is too volatile and your emotions too out of control. If you want to sail away from here then you have to learn how to control yourself or else you'll set the whole ship on fire while we are at sea. Do you understand?" Kaywinnet stated seriously looking directly into Sarafina's distressed face.

"I understand," Sarafina stated quietly. She was afraid of her fire; she couldn't control it. She startled a bit when she felt Rhoswen's hand slide into her own but felt her body relax at the contact. If Rhoswen was there, she could handle it.

"Now, there is a woman who has a crew of people who are like us. I don't know if she is in port right now, but it wouldn't hurt to ask," Kaywinnet stated after she had thrown her backpack over one shoulder. Seeing that Albert was done she whistled for him to come down. Once again he landed on her outstretched arm.

"Now listen, you. You can stay here until we find a ship. When we do, I'll call for you, and don't give me that look. You can stay here without me if that is what you want," Kaywinnet scolded her friend. He cried out in agitation at the suggestion, to which Kaywinnet smiled in return.

"Good, be gone then. I don't know how long this will take."

With another shrill cry, Albert took off back into the forest.

"Will he be able to hear you if he is in there?" Rhoswen asked.

"Oh sure, my whistle may not seem loud to you, but the sound carries a lot farther than what you hear. Come along," Kaywinnet replied. Both girls exchanged a bemused look before quickly catching up to Kaywinnet's retreating form. There was a lot more to their friend than met the eye.

~~~

"Adrian, would you stop acting like a fool and hurry up," Hine called as he stood on the dock outside of Nadia's ship waiting for his son. Said son was currently down the dock a bit talking to a barmaid at the pub. Adrian shot his father an embarrassed look before making his excuses and hurrying over to his side.

"Kindly refrain from calling me a fool, father," Adrian stated once he reached his side. He ducked quickly as Hine made to smack the back of his head.

"Kindly stop acting like one. Stalling is not going to stop you leaving, so you might as well suck it up and get onto the ship," Hine stated testily. He hated sending his son away, but he hated his recent informant's news more. The twins with the powers he had been waiting for had disappeared. Thena's hold on their family was truly lax if such an event could have happened right under her nose. Hine was still fuming about it, and he was also swamped with a bit of guilt. He had, after all, almost strangled his informant in his fury. The poor man was now resting in one of his guest bedrooms at home, and he was going to have to give him a pay raise.

"Father, Father, Father!" Adrian called. Hine snapped out of his trance to see that Adrian was halfway up the gangplank.

"Sorry, coming."

"Do not feel too bad about Hest…" Adrian started only to be cut off by his father's hand.

"And that right there is why I am sending you away. What is the point of having secret agents if you go saying their names in public? And I do not feel bad. He should know by now to deliver bad news and then run away," Hine mumbled as he passed his son. Adrian chuckled at his father's discomfort. Although he was fairly certain his father wasn't an evil man, he did tend to have more than a few evil tendencies.

"NADIA!" Hine bellowed as he reached the main deck. Within moments, a furious Nadia was pelting down on him. Hine did what any reasonable man would do in the face of Nadia's fury; he ran and hid behind his son.

"Do you have any idea how long I have been waiting here? Two whole days, Hine. TWO! If I get caught because you are a highhanded bastard, I promise you I will break out of jail just to come and kick your ass!" Nadia hissed at Hine's cowering form. She couldn't get to him without hurting Adrian, and though it was the boy's fault that she had been stuck in port an extra two days, she didn't hold it against him. No, it was all his father's fault.

"Nadia, my dear..."

"Don't you *my dear* me. You owe me money, Hine. I had to give up two shipments because of you," Nadia growled. Seeing that he was out of immediate danger, Hine emerged from behind Adrian.

"Hi, aunt Nadia," Adrian stated happily into the pause.

"Hello Adrian, you can go below if you'd like. All the guys are in the galley," Nadia stated as she ruffled Adrian's hair. She smiled in the face of his scowl before turning her attention back to his father as he left.

"How much?" Hine stated with a sigh as he brought out his checkbook.

"£900"

"£900, why that is robbery!" Hine exclaimed even as he started to write out the check.

"What do you expect, I'm a pirate. Robbery is what I do for a living," Nadia stated with a smirk. "What did you want to talk about?"

Hine paused for a moment before raising his eyes to search Nadia's face. He could see that she was still a bit pissed with him, but her question was sincere.

"He can't come back here."

"What do you mean?" Nadia asked, astonished.

"Just what I said. Adrian can't come back here. Not for a long time at least, a year maybe two. I don't want him here when everything starts to fall into place. He could get hurt, and he will undoubtedly get in the way," Hine stated softly as he looked out to sea. It pained him greatly to exile his only son, but he knew it was for the best. Hine had plans, and to complete them he would need to be unhindered by parental urges.

"Where am I supposed to keep him? In case you don't remember, I come back to port every couple of months, I refuse to stay away for a year or more," Nadia stated with a huff.

"Take him to your sister's house. Tell her I sent him. She'll keep him."

"You know Chewy hates him," Nadia stated with a small smile.

"He does not; he just hates the alligator him, and as long as your sister doesn't turn him into an alligator again we should be fine," Hine replied with a snort. He well remembered the story of Adrian's exploits as an alligator when he had accidently insulted Nadia's sister the one other time he had been allowed to travel with her.

"He'll cause all types of mischief," Nadia stated with a sigh. Adrian was going to be crushed when he found out.

"I'm sure he will be fine. I will come later to collect him--when everything is completed. He can take his fury out on me then," Hine replied, handing Nadia her check. With a nod, Hine turned on his heel and left the ship. Nadia watched him disappear into the crowd on the dock and sighed again. Looking down at the check in her hand she cursed loudly before laughing.

"That bastard only gave me £700!"

Chapter 11

Gama and Hilt sat in their large living room and surveyed the people who had gathered. It had been three weeks since Kaywinnet, Sarafina and Rhoswen had disappeared into the forest. Kaywinnet's parents had come at their call, as well as Rayne's parents, a few of Hilt's illusive informants, both of the girls' tutors, and their butler and most trusted helper Yessi. They all stared at each other in silence until Gama could take the silence no longer and decided to start their impromptu meeting.

"As you may have all realized, our girls have gone missing. Hilt and I have come to the conclusion that Sarafina, Rhoswen, and Kaywinnet are all together somewhere, as Yessi saw them all dashing from the house towards the forest. We have had people looking for them for weeks, but so far they have only come across a few burnt trees. The trail goes cold halfway into the forest, which at least means that Sarafina was able to contain her fire enough not to leave a visible trail. However, that leaves us with a big problem as we no longer know in which direction they went," Gama started.

"So it is true. One of your girls does possess the fire affinity," Kaywinnet's mother spoke up. She was a tall woman, willowy with strawberry blond hair. Her face at the moment was grave, and filled with anxiety. She had been calling Gama almost daily for reports after it was discovered that the twins were not the only children missing.

"Yes, Sarafina possesses that trait. They were having their first lesson with their tutors when all of this happened," Gama stated, sweeping a hand through the room to indicate the hole in the floor, and the charred furniture closest to it.

"Sarafina did that?" Kaywinnet's mother stated with a gasp. She was more surprised that they had not gotten the hole fixed, but as she looked at Gama she realized that they had left it there as a daily reminder of their mistakes.

"She was doing very well with her lessons until she became frustrated, and frightened, I think. I tried to calm her down, but she quite literally exploded," Walt stated calmly. He stood up from the chair that he had inhabited and walked to the hole in the floor. He was still impressed by the sheer destruction that Sarafina had wrought…it scared him a bit because the girl had so much power. Without proper training, she would burn out and die in less than four months. It was the main reason her parents were so desperate to have her found.

"Then she must be found. With power that great she will burn out in no time!" Rayne's mother exclaimed. They all turned to look at Gama and Hilt who sat in a contemplative silence. Instead of addressing the issue of the twins, Hilt chose instead to turn to Rayne's parents.

"Do you know what has happened to your daughter?" he asked softly. Both parents shared a look before turning back to Hilt.

"No, although we have an idea," Rayne's father stated gruffly.

"Do you want to share your idea with us? We have an idea ourselves; it would be nice to bounce ideas off each other," Hilt responded.

Rayne's father looked very uncomfortable about sharing his ideas, which led Hilt to believe that their ideas were one in the same.

"If you would follow me to my office, I believe this may be a conversation best had behind closed doors," Hilt stated as he got to his feet. Both Kaywinnet's and Rayne's fathers followed him out of the room. Left alone with the other mothers, Gama suddenly felt the urge to cry.

"You can cry you know. I doubt anyone here would judge you. Our children have gone missing and there is little we can do besides search for them and pray to the Mother for their safe return," Kaywinnet's mother said softly. She had taken Hilt's vacated seat and wrapped an arm around Gama's back. Taking in the warmth and comfort that her old friend was willing to give her, Gama finally broke down. She felt Rayne's mother sit to her other side and the three women cried together. Unbeknownst to them, the other men in the room slipped quietly away, each to their own duties.

~~~

Hilt stood in the middle of his office and paced as the other men settled themselves. Hilt smiled a bit as he noticed that his ladder had not completely found its way back to its proper place. The smile turned into a grimace as his thoughts turned back to his daughters.

"You have asked us here to talk, Hilt––so talk," Lundon, Rayne's father, spoke up after a moment of silence.

"You are correct. It is my belief that Thena is not what she seems. Years of power have corrupted her," Hilt said after a moment of contemplation. Talking about their elder in such a way was a risk, especially if these men were not suspicious of her as he was.

"Then you would not be the only one. Thanus and I," Lundon motioned to Kaywinnet's father, "have discussed the same thing on multiple occasions, especially since Rayne went missing on an assignment that Thena sent her on," Lundon scoffed. He wanted to get his hands on the woman that he was sure was behind his daughter's disappearance. However, it was hard to get close to Thena when you were not part of the Circle of Elders in the English Fold––and to bring up such an allegation in a meeting without evidence would be hard to push through.

"Then we are of one mind. I have a couple of men that I have working in Thena's household," Hilt commented. He pulled a rope, an old relic from when the house was built, and moments later Yessi entered the room.

"How may I help you, sir?" Yessi asked with a small bow.

"Bring in Walt and Mathius, if they have not left already. If they have left, please send for them," Wilt requested.

"At once, sir."

"The tutors are the people you have in Thena's household?" Thanus asked with a scoff.

"Yes, and a few others that they recruited whilst there. You may think it strange to bring the enemy into my house; however, as the saying goes, keep your friends close…" Hilt said with a smirk.

"And your enemies closer," Walt said as he walked through the door. The other men tensed for a moment before relaxing.

"It is a good thing then that you were under my hire before you were under hers," Hilt responded. Walt nodded in agreement before taking a free chair. Mathius had left as soon as the men had left the room and had to be called back.

"Tell us what you know," Hilt commanded. He took a place at his desk and reached for pen and paper. It was time to start putting all of the facts together.

~~~

Sarafina and Rhoswen stood in the shadows next to the pub as they allowed Kaywinnet to go inside and figure out if this mysterious ship captain was in port. They had wanted to go with her having never been in a bar themselves, but she had forbidden it.

"Kit acts a lot like Mom doesn't she?" Sarafina had mumbled as they rounded the corner. Rhoswen had agreed with a small laugh.

"I think she just wants to make sure that we are taken care of. After all, this was a very impromptu trip, sister mine," Rhoswen gently reminded her. Sarafina looked crestfallen for a moment before her face turned stony with determination.

"You did not have to come," she muttered.

"Oh, yes I did. Do not try to convince me that you were alright without me around. If I had not been following you, you would have burned down the whole forest. I was putting out the trees you set on fire," Rhoswen scolded. Sarafina's eyes had rounded at the reminder.

"Alright, so I need a tutor. But I don't want to be separated from you again, Wen. Whoever we get, they need to understand that," Sarafina stated firmly.

"Of course. Oh look, Kit is coming back," Rhoswen stated as she pushed off the wall. Kaywinnet was indeed coming around the corner where the girls had hidden themselves.

"I found her, but we have to be quick. She was supposed to leave two days ago, something has kept her here. I don't expect she will be here for much longer though," Kaywinnet stated as she grabbed her bag from Sarafina's outstretched hands.

"After you then," Sarafina stated with a smile. She was getting excited at the prospect of leaving England, something that should have distressed her, she noted absently. They followed Kaywinnet down the dock until they reached a relatively large ship moored at one of the last spots at the dock.

"Here we go, just let me do the talking for now alright," Kaywinnet stated as they climbed the gangplank. They were greeted by a tall man with blazing red hair.

"How can I help you ladies?" he asked, his deep voice instantly charming all of them.

"We are looking for Captain Nadia's ship. Is this the right place?" Kaywinnet asked hesitantly.

"Aye, what can we do for you? I am Foster, her husband and first mate," the man said with a mock bow. Kaywinnet liked him even more for his silliness.

"We are looking for passage to the Americas if you are headed that way. We have money to pay for passage and if that is not enough, we will do whatever jobs are needed on board to pay for what the money does not cover," Kaywinnet stated quickly. She hesitated for a moment before continuing, "We also need to know if there are any nymphs or fairies on board that could possibly tutor my charges," indicating with her head Sarafina and Rhoswen. Foster stared at her for a moment, stroking his jaw before a large smile crossed his face.

"Let me grab Nadia, and Rubella our resident fairy, and see what we can do for you." With that, he turned on his heel and disappeared below deck.

"Are you sure telling him about us was a good idea, Kit?" Rhoswen asked quietly as they stood waiting.

"It is better for them to know before they let us on board, that way there are no surprises later," Kaywinnet answered just before four people emerged from below deck. Foster was followed by two women and another man.

"Here they are, Nadia," Foster stated. The shorter of the two women stepped forward to inspect the girls.

"You say you can pay, how much have you got?" she asked with a small smirk.

"How much does it cost?" Kaywinnet countered. She was aware of what Nadia did for a living--most people were--and she was not about to give away all of their money if she didn't need to. Kaywinnet could not help but wonder how they made a living using wooden boats. Who did they steal from other than other wooden boats? If they procured passage, Kaywinnet was determined to ask.

"Smart girl, I think £300 should cover all of you," Nadia stated. She may be a pirate, but she was a fair trader.

"Deal," Kaywinnet stated without hesitation. That was much less than she had expected.

"Now what is this about needing some fairies on board?" The other woman spoke up suddenly. The trio turned their attention to the new woman and once again Kaywinnet hesitated for a moment. This time is was Sarafina who spoke up.

"My sister and I are untrained nymphs. We have come into our abilities recently and have yet to be properly trained. Let's just say that I need more training than my sister," Sarafina quickly spoke up.

"What are your abilities?" the woman asked.

"I can control water," Rhoswen stated.

"And I control fire; well I try to control fire, and I have some marginal control over plants," Sarafina finished.

"I see why you need some training; fire is very volatile without your emotions playing a part in it," the woman said with a small laugh. She shared a look with the other man who simply shrugged in return.

"I think we can help you. My mate and I have the same abilities, well some of the same. Either way we should be able to help you both," the woman stated assuredly.

"I have to be able to see Rhoswen!" Sarafina burst out. She couldn't risk them separating them again; she would hate to have another explosion on a wooden boat in the middle of the ocean.

"Not a problem. We will teach you on either side of the deck," the woman stated with another shrug. Sarafina nearly sagged in relief. She exchanged a smile with Rhoswen who looked a bit amused.

"My name is Warren, young lady. I will be your tutor," the man stated with a small smile. Sarafina studied him for a moment before deciding that she liked him.

"And my name is Rubella, hun. You'll be working under me," the woman stated with a large smile. Rhoswen smiled back are her.

"Now if that is taken care of, let me show you to your rooms for the trip," Nadia stated sharply. She turned on her heel and walked away only pausing for a moment to make sure that she was being followed. As they followed her below deck she couldn't help but wonder how Kamali was going to react to the number of people she would be bringing by her place.

'I'll have to warn them about getting on her bad side,' she thought with a small smile. Foster, who was walking next to her, followed her train of thought and shared her smile. Maybe this trip he would get away without receiving any of Kamali's brand of welcome.

Behind them, Sarafina was giddy and could hardly contain herself. Grasping Rhoswen's hand tightly, she observed the ship as they passed by.

"Are you alright?" Rhoswen whispered.

"Better than I have been in forever," Sarafina whispered back. She grinned at Rhoswen who grinned back.

"Let us hope that this plan of yours doesn't get us into trouble," Kaywinnet muttered behind her charges. Both girls grinned back at her. Kaywinnet shook her head in amusement. This was going to be an adventure of epic proportions.

PART TWO

Chapter 12

Hine liked to consider himself a reasonable man. He had things that he would do, and things that he wouldn't do given the circumstances, and all who worked for him knew these things. For instance, he would never kill an informant unless he found out that informant was giving away his secrets. He would, however, hurt an informant if the information being passed along wasn't favorable. His informants had learned to pass along bad news and run. On days, like today, when Hine was in a bad mood they had learned that any bad news would be better left alone.

"Sir, I have a new informant for you," a thin pale man by the name of Yik called out. Hine was deep under his house, an area where no one was allowed to go.

"Coming. Send him to my office," Hine called back. He stood in a secret room pushed into the wall of his basement and cradled a picture frame. It held the only photo of Adrian's mother left in existence; after all Hine's anger was an all-consuming thing. Still, she was the mother of his most beloved son, a son he had just exiled. Sighing, Hine placed the picture frame back on its pedestal and exited the room. He made his way swiftly around the other artifacts in his basement and firmly closed and locked the door behind him.

"So you have brought me someone new. What news does he bring?" Hine asked as he settled behind his desk. The boy that stood before

The Last PyoorBlud

him looked like a sewer rat, covered from head to toe in grime so thick Hine was unsure of what color the boy actually was, as even his hair was matted with grime, although Hine could just make out a reddish tint. He was mildly impressed with the deep red eye color the boy sported, a color he hadn't seen since his grandmother was still around.

"I've been told that you're looking for some powerful nymphs?" the boy asked. His voice was a high sounding thing, giving away his age as nothing else would.

"I am. Have you found some for me?" Hine asked with a small smile. He had sent men out to whisper this rumor and his name more than three weeks ago. It was good to finally get some results.

"Saw three of them leaving for who knows were just a few weeks ago," the boy claimed. It had taken him a while to track down someone who could take him to Hine. He had always been able to tell when non-humans were around; it had kept him out of trouble. He could also differentiate between fairy-folk, nymphs, and elves--something few people could do with just a look.

"What did they look like?" Hine asked now with a frown. Three powerful nymphs leaving England was not what he wanted to hear, and as the boy described the three, Hine's frown deepened.

"BLAST!" Hine shouted as he pounded his fists on his desk. The boy stood frozen, whether by his own fear or by something Hine was doing he didn't know, as he watched a dark cloud begin to hover just over Hine's head.

"Sir, please," Yik called out. If he had known that Hine was already in a bad mood he would have held the boy till morning. Hine took a deep breath and pushed out the last of his anger. It would not do to kill the boy; he could prove to be useful.

"Where did you see them?"

"Just off Port Kimi. They were leaving with a pirate. Don't know the captain's name but her ship is full of...those people," the boy's voice dropped into a whisper.

"Those people? Nymphs?" Hine asked. He had a feeling he knew exactly what ship the threesome had left on.

"No, no nymphs till these three. But fairies, and elves. Well partly," the boy answered. He was starting to get nervous, getting too close to revealing his own non-human state.

"Very well. Yik, clean the boy and bring him back here tomorrow. There are things he needs to know if he is going to be an informant for me, plus his pay will need to be negotiated," Hine said as he turned his chair around so he could look out the vast window that stood behind. "Oh, and boy?"

"Yes, sir?"

"What is your name?"

"Don't have a name, sir. People just call me Russus."

"Well, that is unfortunate, but if you want me to call you Russus I will," Hine said with a small chuckle. The boy Russus simply shrugged in response.

"I don't know no other name, sir. Russus'll do me just fine." With that, Yik placed a hand on Russus's shoulder and guided the boy out of the room. Hine stared out the window in contemplation. The twins leaving was going to cause some problems for him.

~~~

Sarafina woke the next morning and looked across the cabin to see Rhoswen and Kaywinnet sleeping in cots around the room.

"Wen, are you awake?" Sarafina whispered. She watched her sister shift in her sleep, but Rhoswen didn't wake up. Thinking that she might as well get up and start looking around the ship she would be on for the foreseeable future, Sarafina sat up. Getting up quietly she put on her clothing and slipped out of the room. She navigated her way back up to the deck and simply stood for a moment taking in the sights, sounds, and smells. Sometime during the night they had set sail. Sarafina looked out on the crystal blue water and felt a calm that she hadn't felt since before Rhoswen had discovered their powers. The newness of these abilities had terrified her, but not for the reasons the others thought. While she was afraid of her fire getting out of control, she was more afraid of losing herself to these new abilities. Could she still be the same Sarafina when she wasn't even human, as she had originally believed? As Sarafina watched the waves created by the boat she began to feel more like herself again; it was a very welcome feeling.

She stepped to the railing and pushed herself up until her entire upper body was hanging over the waves that sped past. Sarafina opened her mouth and allowed the bubbling laughter to jump forth. She had never felt such an overwhelming feeling of freedom before. As the wind rushed past her face she could not contain her smile, or her need to lean further over the edge.

"You'll fall overboard if you do that," an amused female voice said from behind her. Her laughter cut short, Sarafina lowered herself back onto the deck before turning around. Nadia stood behind her with a small smile gracing her otherwise emotionless face. Sarafina stared at her captain for a moment before grinning at her.

"I've never been at sea before," Sarafina practically gushed. Nadia nodded in understanding, well remembering her first time at sea.

"Well, please be careful. I doubt your caregiver will be too happy with me if I let you fall overboard," Nadia stated before turning on her heel and walking away. She paused for a moment as Sarafina called her name.

"Why do you own and operate a wooden ship?" Sarafina couldn't help but ask. She had been having a hard time figuring out why they would use such old transportation in this day and age.

"When I started out, I moved to a town that lived like it was trapped in the 18th century. I bought this ship off Rubella, who comes from a very different world. In truth, it was easier to adapt to this type of ship than it would have been for me to own a large cruise ship or even a fishing vessel. In time, I just found it easier to live like the people of Port Kimi, and if I do a little pirating on the other people who choose to be like me, well…" Nadia trailed off with a smirk.

She wasn't against people knowing she was a pirate by trade. It was all part of keeping to the authenticity of her hometown. In truth, it was a very lucrative way to make a living, if not a bit difficult on a wooden ship. Seeing that she had given Sarafina something to think about she turned back to her original destination; it was time to take over for Foster, at least until they got further out to sea. She glanced back to see that Sarafina had taken her previous position atop the railing. Nadia held back a laugh as she thought back to her youth when she would do the same thing.

"I'm here to relieve you," Nadia said as she entered the steering house. Foster stood calmly at the helm, his eyes trained at sea. His footing was perfectly balanced as always, and Nadia took a moment before he answered to appreciate his form. They were an odd couple to be sure--her so short and rough, and him so tall and cuddly. It was still surprising to her sometimes that he could be so serious, so fit to head her ship in her absence.

"There is a storm coming," he said as he glanced over at her. Nadia nodded in agreement, she had felt the shift in the air when she had come above deck. Years of traveling in this way made them hyper aware of storms.

"No better time for our little water nymph to practice," Nadia said with a sharp grin. She was glad that they would have Rubella to keep them safe, but it was perfect weather to practice control. Foster nodded to her before leaving to go grab something to eat. As he walked downstairs he was passed by one of the other female guests. The girl's red hair caught him off guard for a moment, simply because it had been a while since they had had another red head on board. She flashed him a quick smile as she passed, which he returned before turning back in search of food.

Kaywinnet was trying very hard not to panic. She knew since they were obviously moving that the ship had left port the night before. That meant that Sarafina had to be on board somewhere. Now she simply had to find the blasted girl.

"SARA!" Kaywinnet exclaimed as she reached the deck. Her friend was in the rigging. Kaywinnet almost collapsed when she saw Sarafina fifteen feet up in the air. She raced toward the rigging and time seemed to slow down. Out of the corner of her eye she saw a boy walking across the deck perpendicular to her, she also saw Sarafina lose her footing and tumble backward. Before the scream could fully escape either girl, the boy had taken four lightning-quick steps forward and had caught Sarafina before she hit the deck.

"Oh my MOTHER!" Kaywinnet screamed as she raced toward the pair. Sarafina looked understandably chastened as the boy that held her scolded her.

"If you don't know what you are doing you shouldn't climb up there," Kaywinnet heard him say to Sarafina as he set her back on her feet. Not wasting any time, Kaywinnet took Sarafina into her arms and proceeded to squeeze her to death.

"The first day, THE FIRST DAY!" Kaywinnet kept repeating as she squeezed tighter and tighter.

"Kit, can't breathe," Sarafina managed to get out.

"I don't care. If it wasn't for...." Here she stopped and turned her attention to the boy who had caught Sarafina. He was still standing nearby, although he had moved out of the way when she had rushed over. He was staring at them with slight amusement in his eyes. Kaywinnet paused for a moment to take in the boy's attractiveness.

"What is your name?" she asked, tilting her head to the side. He grinned at her, and the sight of his deep dimples made her knees quake.

"I'm Adrian," he responded as he quickly gave the hyperactive redhead a once over. She was very busty and had the air of a concerned parent as she cradled the girl in her arms to her chest. He stifled a laugh as he saw the girl in her arms start to flail about as her air was cut off.

"Thank you for catching my stupid friend," Kaywinnet thanked him.

"Hey! I'm not stupid, I just slipped," Sarafina spoke up as she finally extracted herself from Kaywinnet's strong grip.

"And that is why you are stupid. What were you doing up there in the first place?!" Kaywinnet exclaimed as she spun to face her. Sarafina shrank away from Kaywinnet's withering glare.

"Nadia said it was okay," she muttered. She chose not to mention that the other girl in the rigging, Iridessa, whom no one else noticed had been watching her as well. A quick glance up told Sarafina that Iridessa was just as mad at her as Kit. Biting back a sigh Sarafina glanced at Kaywinnet and then quickly away as her friend continued to berate her.

"I don't care. If you had died I would have killed you. Now go back to the cabin before I throw you overboard," Kaywinnet snapped pointing below deck. Sarafina opened her mouth to argue, but the power behind Kaywinnet's glare was too much.

"Fine, I'll go get Wen," Sarafina muttered. She threw one more glance toward the rigging before running off. Kaywinnet watched her go before turning her eyes back to Adrian who was still there.

"Thank you again," Kaywinnet smiled.

"No problem. She seems like a handful," Adrian said with an easy shrug.

"Don't get me started. Of the twins, she is the less levelheaded one. But I love her and her sister dearly, and I would follow them to the ends of the earth," Kaywinnet stated. Adrian stared at her, a bit in awe of her devotion of the two girls he assumed were under her care.

"Are you their nanny?" he asked. Kaywinnet glanced at him in confusion before she started to laugh. As she laughed Adrian felt something tug at his heart, and he absently reached up to rub his chest.

"No, just a very old friend. We have been friends since the twins were in diapers. And so much happened back home, and then when Sara and Wen ran off I just had to follow them," Kaywinnet explained as she caught her breath.

"Oh, is Wen the name of the other sister? Yours is Kit, correct?" Adrian asked remembering the name that Sara had squeezed out as she was being smothered.

"Her name is Rhoswen, and Sara is Sarafina. As for me, my name is Kaywinnet, but the girls have been calling me Kit since they were old enough to speak," Kaywinnet responded. She didn't want to stop talking to Adrian, but she had already let Sarafina out of her sight for too long. If a few minutes could see her falling off the rigging above deck, she didn't want to think of what she could get into below deck.

"I'm sorry, but I have to go check on the girls," Kaywinnet stated with obvious regret.

"I'll follow you. I was just on my way to the galley to get something to eat. You and the girls should join me," Adrian offered. His breath caught as Kaywinnet smiled at him. *What is going on?* he thought as he followed behind her. That day he learned that Sarafina was adventurous and determined to see all that the ship had to offer. Rhoswen was certainly the more levelheaded twin and would follow Sarafina around to make sure she stayed out of trouble. Adrian was secretly sure that she enjoyed the adventures just as much, and both enjoyed making Kaywinnet lose her mind periodically.

"What in the world?" Kaywinnet sighed later that day as she sat in the galley with her head in her hands. Adrian sat at her side and tried to contain his laughter. They had been on deck once again as Sarafina and Rhoswen began their first lessons with Warren and Rubella. Kaywinnet was still a bit in awe over what had happened.

~~~

"Sarafina, you will be working with me. Rhoswen, you will be working with Rubella," Warren stated with a small smile. Sarafina looked a bit uncomfortable.

"I have to be able to see Rhoswen. I'm just not comfortable without her," Sarafina finally commented.

"That's fine. Like I said she will just be down the deck from you," Warren said with a shrug.

"Thank you," Sarafina responded with a smile. She nodded to Kaywinnet and Adrian as they moved aside to watch. She allowed herself to be lead down the deck and listened to Warren as he told her what she needed to do.

"I want you to try to channel your fire, pull at your core until you can feel the fire just beneath the skin. Hold it there for a moment and tell me when you have done so," Warren instructed her. He watched her as she closed her eyes and looked inward. He smiled as he saw the light glow coming from just under her skin.

"Alright," Sarafina whispered as she slightly opened her eyes.

"Hold still," Warren whispered as he leaned close. He raised his hand and held it a few inches above Sarafina's arms. He could feel the heat radiating and he smiled. She just needed to focus more and she would be able to control her fire.

"Move please," Sarafina whispered. Warren looked up to see that Sarafina's eyes were wide. As he watched, her pupils began to dilate and the arm his hand still hovered over began to heat up even more.

"Calm down, Sarafina. You are pulling too much at your core," Warren instructed sternly.

"MOVE!" Sarafina snapped. She was trapped in place, even though she wanted to move around Warren so that she could see Rhoswen, her feet seemed to be stuck to the deck.

Warren jumped to the side and watched in slight awe as Sarafina immediately calmed down. Something told him to glance down and he was surprised once again to see the deck curled around Sarafina's feet, anchoring her in place.

"You can control nature, and not just plants that are still alive, but the very essence of nature," Warren said with a surprised chuckle.

"What?" Sarafina asked as she calmed down. She still felt stuck in one place but once she could see Rhoswen's face, a face that looked very worried for her at the moment, she had started to relax.

"Look down," Warren commanded.

"WHAT THE?!" Sarafina exclaimed as she watched the wood slowly retreat off of her feet. They stared in silence at the deck as Rubella and Rhoswen made their way over.

"What did you do?" Rhoswen asked her stunned sister.

"Apparently I moved the deck, but I don't know how and I don't know why," Sarafina responded still in shock. Warren agreed; it was curious that she would have made the deck hold her in place when she so desperately wanted to see her sister. After the situation had been explained, Rhoswen seemed to come up with the answer.

"You want to beat this need to be with me, so subconsciously you tried to keep yourself from needing me, even if it meant keeping you in place while you freaked out."

"That sounds stupid," Sarafina muttered. She stared at the deck and willed it to move. It didn't.

"It looks like that is just one more thing to teach you. In fact, your friend might be willing to help. She is a nature nymph isn't she?" Warren asked. Both Rhoswen and Sarafina nodded, and Warren made a point to update Kaywinnet of Sarafina's newest ability.

"We knew that I had two abilities. I mean we figured that out back home. So if I have two abilities, then do you?" Sarafina asked Rhoswen a few minutes later.

"Yes," Rhoswen said with a smile. She had actually figured out that she had another ability while she was chasing Sarafina through the forest. When she found that she couldn't bring any more water to her aid, she had swiped a hand in frustration at a burning tree. A strong breeze had extinguished the fire, much to her shock. Because in the beginning she was so resistant to believe that she had any abilities at all, she had not thought to test for anything else after her water had manifested.

"You have another ability?" Sarafina asked in shock.

"Yeah," Rhoswen said as she flicked a couple of fingers at Sarafina. A gentle breeze caused her hair to flutter and her eyes grew even wider.

"Kaywinnet is gonna flip," Sarafina whispered. The girls looked at each other for a moment before bursting into laughter.

Adrian touched her arm gently and brought her back to the present.

"At least you have something else to do besides worry," he said with a smile referring to her inclusion in Sarafina's training. Kaywinnet snorted.

"Now I'm going to worry more!" she said with a sigh. Adrian laughed as Kaywinnet groaned in horror. She couldn't help but think that this was going to be an interesting trip.

~~~

Hine slammed his fist against his desk and glowered at the woman that stood across from him. He had to physically hold himself back from unleashing his full fury on Thena.

"You lost them. How could you lose them when they were right under your blasted nose!" Hine snapped. When Russus had been brought in by Yik, Hine had found out that the twins had apparently left the island. Thena was supposed to have a firm hold over them; that she did not had increased Hine's ire from the moment the news had been delivered to him.

"They were in the control of their parents," Thena said stiffly.

"And who is in control of their parents!" Hine snapped. Thena stood straight and scowled at him. She decided that this was not the time to tell him that she had just been informed from her man that Rayne had never made it to her intended destination. Had she known that she couldn't have made Hine any madder at this point, she would have told him and damned the consequences, or so she thought.

"You are incompetent! And I don't need you anymore," Hine stated in a stony voice. He stood calmly from his desk and moved around until he was standing over her.

"What do you mean?" Thena asked, her voice shaking. Hine smiled as he hovered over her. He basked in her terror for a moment as he settled himself. Looking inward he located the one piece of his mother that he had always known was hers.

"I don't need you anymore," he hissed into her ear. Channeling a power that he hadn't used since his early years, Hine held Thena within his furious gaze. His mother's powers were a thing to behold, and though he didn't use them often, he had learned from an early age what they could do when properly controlled.

Thena was unprepared for the blast of energy that hit her. At first she believed that he had set her on fire, for her skin felt as though it was melting from her bones. Her screams broke the air with such a volume that the servants that worked in the barn outside heard her. When she felt as though death would surely come she began to feel as though he had frozen her where she stood, so cold was she. And when she felt as though she could take it no longer he chose to be a bit merciful, and suddenly she felt nothing.

"Now die," Hine sighed as he slipped a knife between her ribs and pierced her heart. He had used his ability of telekinesis to inflict torture upon her mind before killing her. He wasn't completely without mercy, and long latent bloodline connections demanded that her actual death be painless, so he numbed her body before stabbing her, but he watched the horror and agony cross her features as the life drained from her.

Standing over her body, Hine picked up a silken cloth from his desk and started to clean his knife.

"Vincent, clean this up," Hine ordered the man that stood in the corner throughout the whole ordeal. With a small nod, Vincent moved forward to clean up his master's latest dispatch.

"When you have finished that come get me. I have other things to deal with. However," here Hine paused to sneer down at Thena's body, "it is hard to do anything with something so unsightly here."

"Right away, sir," Vincent said with a nod as he moved past his boss to hoist Thena's body over his shoulder. He left the room knowing that he was probably trailing blood, but he would eventually come back to clean it before calling Hine back into the office.

~~~

Kamali stood on the docks four miles from her home. She was waiting for a ship to come in that was holding a very interesting girl. She also knew that Nadia would be coming soon with a wonderful assortment of people, but they would come later. She bit her lip a little as she noticed that Chewy had followed her from the swamp. He was such a puppy.

"Come on, come on," Kamali pouted as she looked out toward the horizon and willed the boat she was waiting for to make an appearance.

"Why are you out here?" Phina asked, coming up behind her. Kamali shrugged and waved her friend away.

"I am waiting for an answer, you know," Phina stated as she came to stand next to Kamali on the dock. She paused for a moment when she saw a pair of familiar eyes in the water under them before turning her full attention back to her friend.

"I am waiting for a ship."

"Yes, I can see that. Otherwise I'm not sure what you would be doing on the dock. If you were going to be out here why did you tell me that I needed to come into town and get food? You could have picked up what we need before you came back," Phina huffed.

"I'm going to have to convince the girl coming on this ship that she has nothing to fear," Kamali said. She absently pulled some meat out of her pocket and dropped it into the water below her.

"Why, what's wrong with her?" Phina asked quietly. She was not even a bit surprised that Kamali was carrying meat in her pockets. Chewy could get his dinner on his own, but his mother was constantly spoiling him.

"I believe that she is Madric's other half. Which doesn't make any sense because from what I can tell she is another nymph hybrid. I don't sense any fairy in her," Kamali responded. Phina stared at her with wide eyes. They both knew that Madric would be waking up soon; after all, it had been many centuries since he had been put under. The spell his mother had put on him was only supposed to last as long as she lived, and her life force had been fading fast in the last few years.

"Well, Madric is very special. Maybe he defies the Mother's rules," Phina muttered. In truth, one of her skills was the ability to tell when someone's perfect mate was close by, or in Kamali's case, if they had already been met. Kamali had already met her perfect match, a dark-and-light fairy hybrid named Raoul.

"I wouldn't doubt it, but I feel as though there is more to this girl than meets the eye. However, since I have yet to meet her I don't really know," Kamali said as she once again bit her lip. Just as Phina was going to comment, Kamali took a quick step closer to the edge of the dock, her eyes focused ahead.

"I guess I should leave you now," Phina said quietly as she turned to leave. However, before she could move more than a step away her wrist was captured.

"No stay, you can tell me if I'm right. Can you feel that?" Kamali whispered. Her body was practically vibrating with the amount of the Mother's gift she could feel coming their way.

"Can I feel…?" Phina tapered off as she felt a massive wave of energy. She held in a gasp only because other things were assaulting her at the same time. Madric's energy was pulsing, as if the surge of energy that she had just felt from the horizon was calling out to him.

"You don't need me to stay here. They are connected for sure. I have to go check Madric," Phina gasped out as she turned away. There was too much power in one place. She needed to distance herself. Kamali stood in shock as she felt the twin powers buffeting against her.

"Merciful Mother."

Chapter 13

Hilt paced back and forth in his office as he thought about what one of his informants had just told him. The spy that he had placed in Thena's house had reported that the mistress of the house had not returned home from a "business trip" that she had left on more than two weeks ago. It made everything that Hilt had been thinking come into stark reality.

"Hilt?" Gama asked as she walked into the room. She held cups of coffee in her hands, the rings under her eyes speaking to the many sleepless nights she had experienced. Seeing her husband's agitation gave her pause.

"Come sit down, dearest. I have news," Hilt said gravely. He watched with heavy eyes as Gama set the cups down and came to sit in front of her husband's desk.

"What news do you have?" Gama asked almost breathlessly.

"I believe that Thena has been killed," Hilt stated. Gama stared at him for a moment in shock before surging to her feet.

"Are you sure?!"

"I have no concrete proof, but the people I have watching her have lost track of her for two weeks now."

"But that doesn't mean she is dead," Gama stated as she bit into her thumbnail, a horrible habit that she had picked up in the months that the girls had been missing.

"You felt that pain last week the same as I. Only those of us truly connected will have felt it. I checked with Kaywinnet's parents and with Rayne's. They all felt the same sharp pain, which only happens when one of the elders dies--the same way it did when Elder Jin passed," Hilt gently reminded his wife. Elder Jin had been Gama's tutor and she had shared a very close bond with him. Gama stared at him for a moment before sinking back into the chair.

"If she is dead, how are we going to find the girls?" she whispered in despair. They had been tracking Thena's movements, sure that she would lead them to their children.

"We will just have to try something else," Hilt stated as he came to throw an arm around her shoulders. He held her silently as she buried her face into his shirt and cried. He vowed to himself once again that he would find their missing children, not only for his own peace of mind but to make sure that his wife never cried like this again.

"We will find them, I promise."

~~~

Russus stood in front of Hine's desk and tried not to squirm. He had been given a spying job, something that he already did without thought, and was told to follow around certain people. One of the people was a Mr. Hilt, apparently the father of the two girls he had seen leaving on the boat. He had new information for Mr. Hine, only the man had yet to show up. Yik had made him go to the office and *Not touch a thing* for nearly an hour. Just as he was about to leave and come back later, a door opened.

Hine stepped out of one of the many secret passages that led from his office to various places in the house and paused at the sight of Russus.

"You are back."

"Yes, sir. You told me to come back if I learned anything I thought you should know. Well, I learned something you should know alright," Russus bowed his head.

"Take a seat. Tell me," Hine commanded waving toward the chair situated in front of his desk.

"Sir, the man Hilt is trying to find his daughters."

"I know this already Russus," Hine sighed. He understood that the boy was young. In fact he usually waited for his informants to reach fifteen before he sent them out into the field, but Russus had the unique ability to get into anywhere without notice and out the same way. It was an invaluable trait to have right now. Hine also suspected that he could identify any non-human people he came across, another invaluable trait. Of course, right now it was still only a suspicion.

"Sir, he has tracked them down," Russus quietly said.

Hine sat up straight and leaned across his desk. His eyes had taken on a nearly manic light.

"Where are they?"

"The man who came to tell Hilt where they were said that they had headed to the mainland, New Orleans to be specific. He said that the boat that they got on came from the town called Little Rock, or Port Kimi just east of where Hilt lives. The town is backwards, sir. It's also where I was found, I suspect you know," Russus took a breath only to be waved on impatiently by Hine. "The ship is captained by a woman who has a relative in New Orleans, a swamp witch that she visits when she goes there."

Hine stopped breathing for a moment when he realized that the twins had somehow boarded the same boat as Adrian. He must have missed them by less than a day. And they would be going to Kamali's for sure. He had suspected that Nadia had taken them, but to have verification was frustrating at best.

"Thank you, Russus. Go tell Yik to get you something good to eat," Hine said with a small smile. Russus nodded and escaped the room so quietly that Hine would have missed his exit if he hadn't been watching.

"I must go on a trip, it would seem," Hine muttered to himself.

There were some things that had to be dealt with before he could leave, but he would be leaving.

~~~

"Now channel the energy and shoot it straight up," Warren instructed Sarafina from his perch on an overturned bucket. He watched as she pulled on her core and created a fireball between her hands. When she deemed it big enough, she threw it into the air. Warren couldn't help but smile when she caused it to explode with just a snap of her fingers.

"Very good, you are getting much better at control," Warren stated as he came to stand before his charge. He made sure to stand off to the side so that she could see her sister across the deck. Sarafina had been serious when she had said that she always needed to be able to see Rhoswen. Both remembered what had happened the first time she had not been able to see her. They hadn't made that mistake again. Sarafina had increased her control exponentially with both her fire and her nature abilities. Kaywinnet had been the most patient teacher, and her teaching style closely mimicked Warren's. Warren could hear Rubella instructing Rhoswen down the deck.

"Now, pull the wind toward you and channel it into a ball," Rubella instructed Rhoswen. They had gotten along wonderfully from the very start. Rubella's upbeat attitude had reminded Rhoswen of her sister and had put her at ease. Rhoswen followed her instructions and pulled at the wind that she felt. They had found through trial and error that if she didn't try to create wind when there was none, she would be able to produce a lot more. Feeling a bit playful, Rhoswen created her wind ball, and instead of throwing it into the air she launched it down the deck at her sister and Warren. Rubella nearly fell over in laughter as she watched the two fall over from the gust of air.

"Oh, you are on!" Sarafina replied. As she got to her feet, she reached for the newest of her abilities. She smiled as she heard Rhoswen and Rubella cry out when the deck beneath their feet shifted and dumped them onto their rears.

"Well, we can't let that stand. Rhoswen attack!" Rubella cried out as she regained her footing. Rhoswen smiled and closed her eyes. Sarafina knew what she was about to do, and started to run for the lower deck. Warren, who was also aware of what was about to happen, chose to block off the entrance to the lower deck by grabbing the back of Sarafina's shirt.

"WARREN!" Sarafina whined as she looked over her shoulder at her tutor. He simply smiled at her as she glared at him.

"Those who work together, go down together," he said simply as he turned to face the oncoming storm. Sarafina spun to face him, only to shy away when she saw the huge wave that her sister had created. She only had time for a small "eep" before they both were covered with frigid seawater.

Warren stood laughing at his pupil as she sat sputtering on the deck. Warming up one of his hands he dried himself off, and then turned to help Sarafina. Her control over fire was getting much better, but he still didn't trust her to not set her clothing on fire.

"What is going on here?" a stern voice cried over the commotion. Kaywinnet stood at the top of the steps, hands on her hips. Adrian stood behind her with a large grin on his face. In the past two months that they had been at sea he had gotten to know his female crewmates very well. Sarafina and Rhoswen were the most interesting twins he had ever met. They were opposites in every way, right down to their abilities. Kaywinnet was a fierce protector; she was also the kindest woman he had ever known. In fact, he had been fighting his attraction to her almost from the moment he met her.

"We were just having a bit of fun, Kit," Rhoswen said happily. She was watching Warren dry her sister off with a small smile. She knew that Sarafina was slightly smitten with her tutor, but she also knew that

Warren and Rubella were practically the same person. She hoped that Sarafina understood that.

"Fun or not, you better make sure you clean up your mess or Nadia is going to have your head," Kaywinnet said with a small shake of her head. She glanced over her shoulder and saw Adrian's huge smile, causing her to elbow him in the ribs.

"Don't encourage them," she scolded with a smile. Adrian simply shrugged without remorse.

"I think we are done for today," Warren stated as he finished drying Sarafina off. She nodded in agreement and made her way over to Rhoswen. Having gotten permission from Nadia to do as they liked as long as they didn't break her ship, the twins ran to the rigging. After her initial scare, Sarafina loved heading up into the rigging. Rhoswen followed her up if only to keep an eye on her more adventurous twin. They had become fast friends with the deckhand Iridessa. The girl was only a year older than the twins, and the three had taken to playing tag in the rigging. Iridessa had taught the girls how to twine their feet into the ropes as a sort of safety net from falling.

Warren and Rubella walked over to Kaywinnet and Adrian to talk about the twin's progress. They all talked amicably and watched the twins play in the rigging like a group of doting parents. Warren and Rubella had discussed late at night if Kaywinnet and Adrian knew that they acted like a couple. Rubella bet they would get together before they got to Kamali's, but Warren, who had seen how much Adrian was trying to resist the attraction, had bet that they wouldn't be together until at least a week after they got to Kamali's. Warren was currently winning their bet.

"I need to talk to you all," Nadia suddenly stated as she appeared behind the group. They all turned to look at the girls simultaneously. Nadia laughed and after assuring them that Iridessa would watch the girls they all headed below deck. When they had all gathered around the long table in the galley Nadia stood in silence at the head for a moment.

"There are some things that I need to tell you that I haven't been honest about until now. Some of the things that I have to tell you will affect us all, some only a few of us," she paused as if to collect her thoughts.

"The first thing that I should tell you is that we will arrive at Kamali's island in the next couple of weeks if the wind holds up. This is good and bad depending on what you think of what I am going to say next," Nadia paused for another second. Her frequent pauses were starting to make those gathered uncomfortable. Finally with a heavy sigh she turned to Adrian.

"Adrian your father has banished you from your home for at least a year's time," Nadia stated flatly. Adrian looked confused for a moment before his face morphed into one of pure fury. Along with that fury came black flames that erupted from his hands and raced across the table.

"SHIT!" Rubella exclaimed as she pulled water from the sink to put out the flames. Kaywinnet stared in awe at the black flames that still swirled around Adrian's head like a demonic halo.

"So what, I'm supposed to stay with Kamali for a year or more? I don't have to go back home on your ship. What is to stop me from going home on any ship that will take me?" Adrian spat out. He was trying to control his fire, an element that he very rarely used. In fact, the last time that his fire had gotten out of hand was when he had been very angry about something.

"You know as well as I that your father has ways to keep you from coming home. I'm telling you this because I care about you, Adrian. You have to be prepared to be away from home for a while," Nadia stated. She had protested from the beginning, but Hine had been absolute in his orders. Adrian stood up and stormed from the room, leaving slightly smoking footprints in his wake. As Nadia began to mutter about someone burning footprints into her floor, Kaywinnet rose from her seat and followed Adrian. He hadn't gone above deck again; instead he had headed further into the ship. She simply followed his footsteps until she got to the brig. There she found him standing in the middle of the room.

"Adrian," Kaywinnet started.

"No, don't! You left home. Yes, you didn't want to go, but you had a responsibility to Rhoswen and Sarafina...you weren't tricked into leaving," Adrian snapped. He was breathing deeply, and slowly. Kaywinnet watched as his fiery halo disappeared.

"You're right. I wasn't tricked. I still want to help you," Kaywinnet responded as she cautiously approached him. When she reached his side she simply rested her head on his shoulder. She said not a word and chose to simply hold him when he finally broke down.

Adrian tried to keep it in, but feeling Kaywinnet rest against his shoulder--a silent comfort--made him break down. Turning to gather her into his arms, he buried his face in her shoulder and cried. He was angry, yes, but he was also scared. His father was his only family; his mother dying in childbirth and his grandparents were not talked about. Being told that he would not see his father for a year or more, to be banished from his home, it was heartbreaking. As he sobbed, he heard Kaywinnet hush him as she brushed her fingers through his hair. Adrian knew he was falling for her. He also knew that this was not the right time to do something about his feelings, but he needed it. Lifting his head, he stared into Kaywinnet's eyes as she smiled at him. He stood still as she gently removed his tears and cupped his face tenderly in her hands.

"There you go. I've got you," she whispered. Instead of answering her, he simply dipped his head and kissed her. It was gentle, and sweet, and perfect, and Adrian smiled a bit as he felt her melt in his arms. Too soon, he pulled away to assess what had just happened. Kaywinnet stood silently in his arms looking up at him with something akin to wonder on her face.

"Probably not the best time to do that," Adrian said after a moment.

"Well…" Kaywinnet started and then it was like her mind caught up because her face burst into a blush so fierce Adrian was surprised she didn't pass out.

"Kit?"

"I'm sorry!" Kaywinnet exclaimed before jerking from the embrace and racing up the stairs to the higher levels. Adrian was left standing in bewilderment before he burst into laughter. He wasn't offended by her leaving because he had seen her face; she wanted him just as much as he wanted her.

~~~~

"This was a horrible idea," Rayne said as she stood on deck looking toward the shoreline that was slowly getting closer. Kinta stood at her side and smiled at her hesitation. When she had found out that they were less than three days from Kamali's, Rayne had become so excited that she had stirred up the sea and almost caused an accident.

"Why do you say that?" Kinta asked as he leaned on the railing next to her. He angled his body so that he could see her properly and smiled at her face. Rayne looked as if her doom were approaching.

"I just feel like this was a horrible idea. How about I just stay with you guys instead of getting off?" Rayne mused with a frown. She was looking at the shoreline intently, trying and failing to pinpoint the source of the pull that she was feeling. She had been feeling like someone was pulling at her soul since the night before.

"It will be fine. Besides, you want to get back to England and track down the woman who kidnaped you right? Well we won't be going back anytime soon, so you better take your chance now before it's too late," Kinta replied with a pat to her back. He had grown fond of Rayne in the three months that she had been on board, almost like a little sister.

"Revenge helps no one," Rayne replied. She did want to go home, to see her parents and Kaywinnet again, but the anger toward Thena had all but vanished.

"You are wise beyond your years, but you can't stay here forever. Whatever is worrying you is sure to be nothing in the end," Kinta smiled at her.

"I hope so," Rayne responded. She stayed where she was as Kinta left to help the rest of the crew bring them ashore. She kept up the slight breeze that was gently bringing them in, but her thoughts were unsettled. As she stood there she saw a figure standing at the edge of the dock they were approaching. The woman was dressed in a long skirt with a long-sleeved flowing top kept closed by a vest. She was also wearing a cloak that trailed out behind her and down toward the water. Rayne thought she must be burning in the heat, but she looked calm. A bit of movement in the water caught her eye and Rayne was surprised to see a gator swimming in lazy circles below the dock. Turing her attention back to the woman again Rayne allowed herself to relax a bit and reach toward her. The woman flared up like the sun and Rayne was surprised by the amount of power that was within her.

"Who is she?" Rayne asked out loud. She did not expect an answer and so was surprised when Kinta responded.

"That is Kamali, the woman we are all here to see."

"How did she know we would be in today?" Rayne asked with a raised eyebrow.

"She didn't, and yet she did––mysterious woman. I have learned to expect anything and everything from her."

Rayne nodded in agreement before the tugging grew to be too much. Without knowing what she was doing, she allowed her abilities to soar. She did her best to keep everything contained but knew that it didn't work very well. The men were taken unaware as she pulled water on board to circle her, propelled by the wind that created a cyclone around her. The deck shook under their feet and the two lanterns that smoked flared to life.

"RAYNE!" Kinta cried out from just outside her watery prison.

"Get back!" Rayne called, but she doubted he heard. The pull was lessening as she allowed more and more of her abilities to leak out. Finally, she felt ready to pull them back into her core, the resulting decrease causing her to fall to her knees.

"What was that about?" Kinta asked as he came to stand by her side.

"I have felt a tugging at my soul since last night. Finally it became too much and I just had to let it out. Did anyone get hurt?" Rayne asked as she looked around hesitantly. It didn't look as though there had been any damage, but the crew did look pretty shaken up.

"No one got hurt, but I must admit you did scare us all," Kinta said with a small chuckle. They lapsed into silence as the ship finally pulled up to dock. As the gangplank was lowered, the woman dashed aboard.

"Are you alright?" she exclaimed as she drew closer to Rayne.

"I'm fine," Rayne said as she shuffled away from the woman. Although she didn't look that much older than Rayne, Rayne knew that she must be very old to have so much knowledge in her gaze.

"I know you may be wanting to stay with the ship, but I think it would be better for everyone if you came with me," Kamali said in a rush. Her heart was still pounding after seeing the girl's powers on such a large-scale display.

"I don't know what you are talking about," Rayne said with suspicion. She had seen the woman board the ship and come right to her; she had talked to no one…so how did she know about her doubts.

"Of course you do," Kamali said with a sigh. She had known that the girl was going to be difficult. Taking her hand in her own Kamali focused for only a moment. She was surprised to feel the consciousness of Madric lingering just outside the consciousness of the girl, Rayne.

"I can tell you what the tugging is," Kamali said with a small smile. She just kept from laughing when the girl's mouth dropped open in surprise.

"How did you…?"

"I can feel it when I touch you," Kamali responded. She wasn't surprised when Rayne pulled her hand from her grip.

"Who are you?" Rayne asked in shock.

"I am Kamali, and I believe I have much to tell you, Rayne."

Rayne stayed silent for a moment not even surprised that this strange woman knew her name before sighing. The tugging was beginning to get assertive again and Rayne knew that Kamali could help her.

"Alright, lead the way."

Chapter 14

Anyone who didn't know Rayne would think that she was calmly taking in her surroundings. However, Rayne was not calm in the slightest. As they traveled further into the swamp her heartbeat was beginning to skyrocket and her hands were shaking.

"There is no need to be nervous," Kamali said with a gentle tone. She even went so far as to rest a hand on Rayne's arm, only to have the arm jerked from her grasp.

"I'm not nervous, I'm terrified!" Rayne snapped. Kinta laughed a bit at her voice but quieted when she sent him a hard glare. In truth, the closer they got to the island that Kamali inhabited the worse the pull had become. Kamali had told her not to fight it, but she was terrified of letting go again on such a small boat.

"If you need to let go then let go. Concentrate on the pull and everything will be directed up instead of out," Kamali said after a moment of watching Rayne. She knew that the girl was wary of her, something that she couldn't help even if she wanted to, but if she kept it all bottled up she was going to explode.

"Focus on the pull?" Rayne asked slightly panting. The pull was getting stronger by the moment, pulling at her the same way it had on the ship.

"Focus on the pull," Kamali repeated. She watched as Rayne closed her eyes with a sigh and started to breathe deeply. The fire in the single lantern that hung from a pole at the front of the boat began to grow in intensity; the wind around them picked up slightly and the waves of the river became choppier. Kamali calmly brushed aside the branch of a tree that was reaching out for them from the banks as she continued to watch Rayne. When the pull receded she opened her eyes and smiled.

"Everyone alright?" she asked hesitantly.

"Oh sure, if you don't mind grabby tree vines everyone is fine," Kinta responded as he tried to remove a vine that had curled around him as they passed. Rayne stifled a chuckle as she watched him struggle and turned slightly less suspicious eyes at Kamali.

"You were right," she commented softly.

"I tend to be," Kamali responded with a small smile. They were silent for the rest of the ride to Kamali's island. When they reached it, they were told to stay in the boat while Kamali went inside her house and grabbed a few things. She returned swiftly and turned the boat further into the swamp.

"I thought we were going to your house," Rayne commented as they headed further in.

"And so we did, and now we are going to Madric," Kamali answered with a wry smile.

"Who is Madric?" Rayne asked as she felt a new sensation. It was no longer a tugging but a gentle caress against her soul.

"He is the one calling out to you. I expect he is happier now that you are getting closer to him," Kamali responded with a tilt of her head. It looked as if she were listening for something. They traveled in silence for a moment more before Rayne gasped and Kamali chuckled. They had reached Madric's water, the clear crystal blue a stark contrast to the murky swamp water they had been traveling through. Here the vegetation grew wild and free, beautiful colors that called out to you and welcomed you in. Rayne had never seen such a beautiful place and she was in awe.

"What is this place?" Kinta asked into the silence.

The Last PyoorBlud

"This is Madric's realm, I suppose you could say. He feeds his energy into his surroundings. This has been the result," Kamali responded. She watched as Rayne dipped a hand into the water and pulled out a frog. The animal sat patiently in her hand as she stroked its head, and croaked loudly at her as she put it back into the water. They finally came to the dock on Madric's island and Rayne was the first off. She began striding toward the modest dwelling only to be stopped by another woman coming out from inside.

"Who are you?" Rayne demanded. The caress was becoming a small pull again as she stood just outside the source.

"I am Phina. Who are you?" Phina responded with a slight smile. She had been sitting with Madric, soaking up the energy that he was pushing out in waves. She hadn't been so connected with the boy since they had first brought him to the swamp and his magic had made it safe for them to inhabit it.

"I am Rayne, and I need to see Madric," Rayne responded. She waited for a moment before adding a small, *please*.

"Go on," Phina stated as she moved aside. Rayne entered the house and allowed the pull to bring her to the room in which Madric lay.

"He's asleep?" she asked in amazement as she stared down into the boy's perfect features. She felt the pull growing and so she moved closer until she could rest a hand upon his shoulder. At the contact, she was so overcome with a feeling of joy and peace that she collapsed into the chair at his bedside.

"What..." Rayne gasped as she tried to recover from the feeling. Her abilities were swirling just under the surface and she could feel an answering pull in the boy beside her.

"Madric sleeps due to a spell his mother placed on him long ago. I believe you are his perfect mate, his one true other half," Kamali said as she walked into the room. Rayne stared at her for a moment before turning to look back at Madric.

"Okay," she whispered before slumping forward in a faint. Kamali tutted softly at the poor girl before picking her up and placing her on the bed next to Madric. They would need to stay in contact for a while she was sure. Now they would wait for the others to join them; it wouldn't be long now. Kamali predicted that they would be joining them before the week was out, and with that thought she turned back to the boat to head back to her house. There were many things to be done before the rest arrived.

~~~

Sarafina and Rhoswen stood at the bow of the ship and looked toward the fast approaching shoreline. Kaywinnet stood a bit behind them with a small smile gracing her otherwise stiff features. It had been eleven days since she had comforted Adrian, and she was doing a great job of avoiding him on the small ship.

"I can't believe we are almost there," Sarafina said with a sigh. It had been a long trip; three months of self-discovery and companionship had changed the way that Sarafina viewed her abilities. Rhoswen had come out of her shell and was climbing the rigging almost as much as Sarafina.

"What do you plan to do after we meet Kamali?" Rhoswen asked. They hadn't come on this ship with much of a plan, just get away from home and find someone to teach them how to use their abilities. Now that they were finally reaching their destination, Rhoswen was unsure of how they would proceed.

"I was just thinking that we could explore this country a bit. I'm sure Kamali can point us toward others like us. Maybe it would be a good idea if we expanded our knowledge," Sarafina responded as she turned to lean back against the railing. Her pale skin had developed a nice tan and it made her white teeth seem that much whiter. Kaywinnet snorted at her suggestion, bringing the attention to herself.

"You have a better idea?" Sarafina asked with a smirk.

"No actually, but the idea of trying to find others like us on the continent is a daunting one. This place isn't like the Island, the Americas are three times as big with many places to hide," Kaywinnet explained.

"That's true, but I don't want to go home yet," Sarafina said with a sigh.

"We should inform your parents of our whereabouts as soon as we get to Kamali's island," Kaywinnet stated. She neglected to say that she had already written a general letter and had plans to send it on the first ship she could find once they landed. In her head she knew that Sarafina and Rhoswen should write to their parents, but in her heart she knew that they wouldn't without some cajoling.

"Do we have to?" Sarafina asked with a pout. In truth she didn't want to tell her parents where they were; given how she and her sister had left, she knew they would immediately come to find them. And while the journey was long enough for them to disappear before their parents arrived, she knew that they would follow. She also knew her parents would not take the slow form of travel of a wooden ship, but would most likely take the first plane over. Sarafina had realized that she loved the simplicity of the olden days when journeys took months to make and everything simply slowed down to accommodate them.

"Yes," Kaywinnet said with a smile. Sarafina went to say something else before catching sight of someone over Kaywinnet's shoulder.

"ADRIAN!" Sarafina exclaimed bouncing over to him. She missed Kaywinnet stiffening again, but Rhoswen did see and sent a sly smile at her oldest friend.

"Hello, ladies," Adrian said as he walked slowly toward them. He was trying not to laugh as he took in Kaywinnet's stiff features.

"Kit, how are you?" he asked as he walked up behind her. He held in a laugh as he watched her ear turn red.

"I'm fine, and you?" Kaywinnet asked. She cursed her voice as it squeaked. She hadn't been able to look at Adrian much less talk to him in days.

"I'm glad to hear that. Nadia says that we will be docking soon. After we dock we will be taking another boat further into the swamps to get to Kamali," Adrian informed them. They nodded their understanding, and Sarafina and Rhoswen left to make sure all of their things were packed.

Kaywinnet stood in tense silence as Adrian turned all of his attention on her.

"You can't avoid me forever," Adrian whispered.

"Obviously," Kaywinnet said with a small laugh. They stood in silence for a couple minutes more before Adrian reached out to brush a curl of hair behind her ear.

"I think we have some things that we need to talk about, the least of which is that I desperately want to kiss you again," Adrian said with a crooked grin. Kaywinnet blushed at his words but smiled.

"Alright let's talk."

~~~

Hine sat in his office and pouted. There really was no other word for what he was doing. As he sat there his mouth pulled into a deep frown, the only sound that could be heard was the slight tapping as he drummed his fingers on his desk. The entire room still smelled of bleach; of course that was because his man had had to clean it again yesterday. He was running out of informants. Maybe his temper was getting a bit out of control. With that thought, Hine moved to his liquor cabinet and poured himself a finger of scotch.

"Sir," Vincent called from the doorway. He had just finished disposing of his boss's latest informant and was slightly wary to approach him.

"Yes?"

"I have some news that I think you would benefit from hearing," Vincent replied as he slowly entered the room. Once he stood in front of Hine's desk he waited for the signal to proceed. It was a while before Hine waved a hand at him, his mind preoccupied on other things.

"The girl Rayne has been spotted with Kamali," Vincent stated calmly. He watched as Hine's eyes, which had previously looked a bit vague, sharpened and he turned his full attention to his manservant.

"How do you know this?" Hine asked, his voice dangerously low. Vincent's muscles tensed as he prepared to run as soon as his news had been delivered.

"I had a man stationed there after it became apparent that that was where you were going to send young Adrian. His report only got to me now, and he used the fastest falcon he had, so she must have just arrived a few days past," Vincent answered, choosing not to say that he was disgusted at the slow method of communication that his informant had chosen to use. There were still so many people who refused to keep up with the times.

"She was supposed to be dead!" Hine snapped as the crystal decanter in his hand cracked.

"It would seem that the twins were not all that Thena had lost," Vincent said with a frown. He waited a moment before turning on his heel and exiting the room. As he closed the door he heard the decanter smash against the far wall. With a sigh he went to fetch the cleaning supplies from the kitchen, all the while thinking that he should just have them moved upstairs to the closet outside of Hine's office.

Chapter 15

Kamali looked up from the pot of chili that she was making with a smile. She had just heard a yelp come from outside her door and it made her smile to know that Adrian had returned. She set the fire to a lower setting so that her food didn't burn and hurried outside. She nearly doubled over laughing as she took in the commotion that was happening at the end of her dock. Nadia, Foster, and two girls that looked to be twins were standing on the end of her dock looking back into the boat they had arrived in with a mixture of laughter and horror on their faces. She joined them to peer into the boat. A very long, very familiar tail was wrapped around the thigh of a petite redhead, while Adrian was trying and failing to unlatch Chewy's jaw from his leg.

"GAH! Chewy get off!" Adrian cursed as he pulled at the gator's nose. In truth, he wasn't being hurt, but anyone would be upset to have an alligator attached to their leg.

"Adrian, what is going on?" Kaywinnet asked as she stared in horror at the tail that was still winding its way up her leg. So far it was covering an entire leg and was now wrapping around her waist.

"This is aunt Kamali's pet, Chewy," Adrian bit out as he finally got Chewy to let go of his leg. His relief was short lived. As he got free and jumped onto the dock Chewy decided to leave, carrying Kaywinnet away with him.

"Wait, what? ADRIAN!" Kaywinnet called out as she was pulled away, boat and all. The others on the dock were laughing as Adrian called that she would be fine. Kaywinnet was not pleased; in fact she was pissed. Taking off the braided root that she always wore on her wrist she channeled her ability into it and created a whip. Leaning back a bit, she flicked the whip into the water where she saw the alligator's body.

"LET GO!" she cried as she whipped the gator. The tail immediately stiffened before sliding off of her body to disappear into the water. As she watched, Chewy's head appeared at the end of the boat. He looked at her with the same intelligence that Albert had.

"I'm sorry, but it isn't very nice to kidnap people. Would you take me back?" Kaywinnet asked as she rewrapped the band around her wrist. Chewy looked at her for a moment more before his tail reappeared. It gently wrapped around her waist and she felt the slight tugging as the boat moved back toward the dock. The rest of them were still standing on the dock. Nadia looked very surprised to see her coming back. Once they reached the dock the tail left her waist and Chewy disappeared further into the swamp. Kaywinnet jumped onto the dock and stood with her hands planted on her waist as she glared at the lot of them.

"Thank you so much for helping me," she said, sarcasm dripping in her tone. Adrian came close to hug her, but she brushed him off. Narrowing her eyes on the only person that she didn't know she stomped over to the woman who was laughing behind everyone.

"YOU! If you can't control your pet you should put it in a cage!" Kaywinnet scolded. Kamali stifled her laughter though her eyes were still alight with amusement.

"Honestly, I think I am his pet rather than him being mine. I do apologize. Chewy is friendly, but sometimes he does get out of hand."

"Well, I accept your apology. I am Kaywinnet. It's nice to meet you," Kaywinnet said with a sigh as she held her hand out for Kamali to shake. Turning, she beckoned Rhoswen and Sarafina forward.

"You two must be Rhoswen and Sarafina," Kamali said with a smile. They nodded though she could tell that they were wondering how she knew their names. "I believe one of your friends arrived a few days ago."

"KIT!" They all turned at the new voice, and Kaywinnet's face lit with joy.

"Rayne!" The girls met in a hug as they babbled at each other. Without thought they slipped into the language they had discovered in their youth.

"Reaaye ouyaye kayoaye, *Are you okay*?" Kaywinnet asked.

"Inefaye, henaTaye oldsaye emaye Iaye inktaye. *Fine, Thena sold me I think*," Rayne responded. She chuckled at her friend's horrified face. They talked for a moment more before Kaywinnet turned to introduce her to the rest of her shipmates. Rhoswen and Sarafina greeted Rayne with enthusiasm, glad to see her safe. Nadia and Foster only nodded in her direction as they were talking in depth with Kamali. Adrian was just as enthusiastic as the twins; he had heard tales of Kaywinnet's best friend.

"So how did you end up here?" Sarafina asked after they had settled in Kamali's living room. Rayne launched into a thrilling tale of kidnapping and escape. It was only when she reached the part where she met Kamali that her voice softened and her eyes became wistful.

"If I didn't know any better, Rayne, I would say that you were in love," Kaywinnet teased. Rayne blushed.

"How did you have time to fall in love?" Rhoswen exclaimed with a laugh. With a bright red face Rayne explained about Madric.

"Well show him to me," Kaywinnet demanded.

"In time," Kamali called from the kitchen. She smiled as she heard groaning from the living room.

"How have you been, sis?" Nadia asked as she walked into the kitchen. Kamali pondered for a moment, as she did every time that Nadia called her sister, wondering if she should be honest about their relation; and as always, decided against it.

"Alright. Phina is starting to go mad again. I keep telling her that she needs to find a man, but she says that her person will come soon enough," Kamali responded with a chuckle.

"Well, she does know these things," Nadia responded. She had never really understood Phina, but she was grateful to her. Without her push she would have never pursued Foster.

"True, very true," Kamali hummed in agreement. They stood together silently as Kamali finished preparing dinner. She would periodically hand things to Nadia who then set them on plates.

"Rayne, dear, would you go get Phina?" Kamali called. Rayne responded with a positive and took Kaywinnet and the twins with her. It was time to meet Madric.

~~~

Phina sat in her place next to Madric and meditated. She had kept watch over this boy for more years than she could count. The distant pulsing of his mother's life force was dimming as each day passed.

"I believe you will be waking up soon, my dear," Phina whispered. Madric's power flared for a moment in agreement.

"Phina! Kamali says to come have dinner with us," Rayne said as she entered the room. She walked over to where Madric slept and gently brushed a strand of hair off of his face. Kaywinnet watched her friend with a fond look. Sarafina was looking around the small house with interest, only mildly interested in the sleeping man. Rhoswen was having a hard time breathing. The woman that sat next to Madric was staring at her with a surprised look.

"Hello," Rhoswen said with a small nod in her direction.

"Hello," Phina responded just as quietly. She was in shock, because the girl standing in her doorway was perfect for her. It had been so long, that Phina was sure that her perfect other half would never show up.

"Phina are you coming to dinner?" Rayne asked as she and Kaywinnet stood to leave. Sarafina appeared next to Rhoswen from somewhere in the house.

"Yeah, I'm coming. Just give me a couple of minutes. Tell Kamali I'll be there in a moment," Phina responded with a small smile. The rest of them left single file, Rhoswen left last, her eyes lingering on Phina. Phina sat in shock as the door closed behind them and sighed heavily.

"Oh Madric, what am I going to do? She is so young, she probably doesn't even know about the Attraction," Phina moaned. She felt so much joy and so much misery at the same time; it was hard to separate the feelings.

She sat there for more than ten minutes before she decided that she had avoided the girl long enough. Resting a hand on Madric's shoulder for a moment she made her way over to Kamali's island. As she approached, she heard the sounds of people, a sound they had been missing for months since the last time Nadia had visited.

"Phina! Come, we saved you a place," Kamali called out as her friend came into the room. Phina made her way over to her usual place and had to bite back a groan. The girl, her girl, was sitting right next to her.

"Let me make introductions. This is Kaywinnet, Sarafina, and Rhoswen," Nadia spoke up, as everyone finally sat down. Phina nodded to each of them as they were introduced, her eyes lingering on Rhoswen's face. Rhoswen looked back and a small smile started to form on her face. Phina could feel a blush creeping up her cheeks and chose to turn away. Unfortunately, that caused her to see Kamali's knowing gaze.

"Shut up," Phina muttered as she dug into the chili.

"I didn't say a word," Kamali smiled. It looked like her friend had found her person at last.

~~~

Lady Matha lay in her bed surrounded by what little family she had left. She was the last of the original nymph's and she was still in wonder over how well their species had grown once they had mingled with the humans. Matha's eyes wondered from face to face and her smile was sad. Her son was not by her side, but it would have been impossible for him to have been. She had sent him away years and years ago for his own safety.

"My lady, it is time," a young woman said as she stood at her side. Matha turned to look at her and smiled. She looked like her sister; she must have been one of her descendants.

"Is it really?" Matha asked quietly. When the girl nodded, Matha sighed. She was dying. She had been dying for the last fifty years and today would be her passing day.

"Are you ready?" the girl asked again. She motioned for the other people in the room to say their goodbyes and vacate the room. They each took a turn to say something to Lady Matha, the only woman who still had the pure powers that came with being a true child of the Mother. She had been part of their village for years, and it was truly a sad day to see her pass.

"I suppose I have no other choice. I only wish that I could see my son," Matha whispered as the last person left the room.

"I have permission to show you," the girl responded, as she quickly helped Matha sit up in the bed. Matha's head snapped to her and her eyes looked hopeful. For many years she had petitioned the elders of the village to allow her to follow her son, if only through the looking glass. The answer had always been no, a punishment for her defiance when the species had been dying.

"They gave you permission?" Matha breathed.

"Yes, though they do not approve of him, they do not think there is anything wrong with granting you this last request."

"Please, please show me my son."

The girl nodded and left the room, only to come back with a large bowl filled with water and herbs. She placed the bowl carefully on Matha's lap and stood back. Matha looked into the water and sent her mind into the water concentrating on Madric. The surface of the water flickered before an image began to appear.

"Oh, my son!" Matha laughed with joy as she took in the sight of her son, now grown and so handsome. He slept as he had done since she had placed the spell on him when he was a baby. She wished that she could see his eyes, but she knew that it was impossible, for he would not awaken until she passed.

"He has grown up so well," Matha laughed as she watched Kamali come into his room. She stared in fascination as she ushered a young woman in. Even Matha could feel the spike in Madric's energy a world away when the girl touched him.

"Oh my, he has a mate," Matha whispered. Her concentration broke as her strength failed her and the image disappeared. Matha sat for a moment and tried not to cry, but she was happy all the same. She had gotten to see her son after so long, and soon he would wake.

"I am ready," Matha told the girl who still hovered at her side. The girl moved the bowl and helped Matha lie back down. She began to say a prayer to the Mother over Matha's body. As she felt her spirit leave her, Matha's last thoughts were ones of joy and hope.

"He will help rebirth this world. Him and all those who love him. They will have a new life, and create a new world."

Chapter 16

Kamali and Phina both stopped talking at the same time. Their eyes widened and Kamali reached out to touch Phina's shoulder. "Did you?"

"Yes, she has passed," Phina whispered in answer to Kamali's question. It seemed that Madric's mother had finally passed. As the thought crossed her mind she began to feel a strong pressure.

"KAMALI!" Rayne shouted as she bolted from the table. Kamali, Phina, Sarafina, and Rhoswen all followed her out of the house. They were barely fast enough to jump onto the boat with Rayne before she propelled them to Madric's island. Rayne could feel the tugging that connected her to Madric grow to a painful level. She could also feel his energy beginning to spike, and the feeling scared her.

Back on Kamali's island Nadia, Foster, Adrian, and Kaywinnet stood on the dock and watched the boat speed away. Kaywinnet couldn't help but worry about her friends, but deep down she knew that she was not needed at this moment. She stood on the dock long after Nadia and Foster had gone back inside, and prayed while Adrian stood by her side.

"What is going on?" Sarafina asked hesitantly. Everyone seemed so stressed that she was afraid to interrupt.

"Madric's mother has passed, and so the spell and binding that she put on him as a baby has broken. It is too much to let out all at once. If we do not do something now, he will destroy the swamp and most of the surrounding area," Kamali responded. She was vibrating with energy, and, fortunately, she knew exactly what needed to be done. As they finally reached the island, she began shouting orders.

"Rayne, go to him, your presence should calm him a bit. Phina, bring the other bed out here, there will be more room. Rhoswen, I need you to find ola leaves; they look like weeds with purple flowers. Sarafina, I need you to help me burn a circle into the ground. GO!" Kamali commanded. The girls snapped into action. Sarafina was the only one hesitant, as she still didn't have complete control over her fire, but she knew how important it was.

Rayne walked into the house and stuttered to a stop as she felt the immense power coming from the room where Madric lay. It took her a moment to gain control of her emotions enough to enter the room.

"Madric, please calm down," Rayne begged as she kneeled next to him. She ran her hands soothingly over his arms and felt his energy settle a bit. As she sat there his energy began to spike again. Rayne prayed to the Mother that whatever Kamali had planned would be ready soon.

Outside, Sarafina and Kamali had finished burning a circle into the ground. While Sarafina used her ability, Kamali had simply grabbed a torch and burned the ground. As they finished, Rhoswen came back into the area with an armful of the ola that Kamali needed.

"Place them at equal intervals around the circle," Kamali commanded as she moved to help Phina bring in a bed from the house.

"Go get him," Kamali requested of Phina as they placed the bed in the precise middle of the circle. Phina nodded and moved into the house. She was only in there for a moment before she came out carrying Madric in her arms followed closely by Rayne. Phina had spent years holding Madric; she was a lot stronger than she looked. She placed him on the bed and stepped back to the edge of the circle.

"Now this is important. We need to keep his powers in the circle. That means that we have to use our own abilities to contain it. Each of you find a place on the circle in between the ola and then think about the ability that you have the most control over. Rayne, pick your strongest; Sarafina, if you can't control the fire, use the earth," Kamali ordered. The girls all nodded and got into position. They all waited patiently, but Madric's rising power was starting to push against them.

"This is the difficult part. You need to focus on your ability but do not use it. Bring it to the surface and reach out to Madric with it. It should correspond with the same ability in him and funnel it into the space between you. I will use my mind to try to connect with him. Everyone ready?" Kamali instructed.

"I'll do earth," Sarafina said after a moment.

"I'll do wind," Rhoswen whispered. She was terrified by the amount of energy she felt from Madric.

"I will use fire," Rayne said, her voice strong.

"I will do water," Phina said after a pause. Water was not an ability that she used often, and deep inside she was afraid that she would lose control.

"On my count, One, Two, NOW!"

~~~

Hine stood at the window of an old castle on the very edge of Suffolk and sighed. Hours ago he had felt an increase in power from the Americas--an energy that he was sure came from the one person that he desperately wanted to find. The child that his mother had abandoned him for; he had been searching for him for years.

"Vincent, I need you to go to America," Hine spoke quietly. He knew that his manservant would always be close by.

"I can be on the first plane headed that way in the morning sir. Is there anything in particular that I am going there for?" Vincent asked as he stepped into the room.

"Find the boy," Hine said with a scowl. Vincent had heard many rants about the boy that had stolen his master's mother.

"How? Sir, I have gone to America many times to find the boy, to find your mother, I have been unable. So what has changed?" Vincent couldn't help but ask.

"I believe that the boy has awakened," Hine said simply. Vincent stood for a moment longer in hopes of more of an explanation, when none came he bowed and left the room. Hine stared out the window and cursed Thena for losing both the girl who could sense the Mother's power in others and the twins who had more power together than anyone else he knew about. He would find them all, and when he did he would find the boy and make him suffer the way that Hine had suffered for over 800 years.

~~~

Madric felt so many people who were just like him but not. As he struggled to contain the power that he felt bursting from every pore, his only thoughts were that he didn't want to hurt anyone. As he struggled to the surface, he felt another presence in his mind.

"*Get out!*" Madric commanded as he pushed at the presence. But it was stubborn and continued to poke at his consciousness.

"*GET OUT!*" Madric shouted as he shoved at the feeling. He felt the other people outside of him buckle under the power he ejected out.

"*Madric, calm down. You know me. Feel me,*" Kamali whispered into Madric's mind. She was having a hard time making contact with him, although it was to be expected. Most people would be resistant to feeling someone else in their mind.

"*Kamali, what is going on?*" Madric asked as he recognized the presence of his caregiver. He knew her voice, remembering the years that she had cooed to him as she and Phina helped raise him from infancy. Knowing that it was her in his mind calmed him down significantly. He allowed the outside pull on his powers to increase until he felt it was manageable.

"*You are waking up. Your mother has passed and so your seal has been broken,*" Kamali explained. When she felt as though Madric was stable enough to retreat from his mind she did. Coming back into herself, Kamali opened her eyes to see how the other girls were holding up. Each girl was sitting on the ground panting from exertion. At some point during their conversation, Madric had gained control of his powers and had stopped projecting outwards.

"Are you all alright?" Kamali asked with a small smile.

"I'm itchy," Sarafina said with a smile. Trying to keep her abilities just under her skin was a weird sensation. The rest of them laughed before Rayne got to her feet and stumbled over to where Madric lie.

"Madric, you should wake up now," Rayne whispered as she pushed aside a lock of hair.

"If you say so," a deep male voice responded. Silence descended in the glade as Rayne began to smile. Madric's eyes fluttered for a moment before opening slowly. His hazel eyes locked on Rayne and he began to smile as well.

"Hello," he murmured.

"Welcome back," Rayne whispered. Kamali and Phina came forward and enveloped Madric in a hug. He was the son they both adored, even though he had been sleeping for what felt like forever.

"Kamali, Phina, thank you for looking after me," Madric said with a smile. He still couldn't move very well, but he knew that movement would come with time. For now he was simply happy to be awake.

Made in the USA
Charleston, SC
12 September 2016